'Can't sleep?'

The Italian's silky voice penetrated her spinning thoughts and Keira could tell from the shifting weight on the mattress that Matteo Valenti had turned his head to talk to her. She swallowed. Should she pretend to be asleep? But what would be the point of that? She suspected he would see through her ruse immediately—and wasn't it a bit of a relief not to have to keep still any more?

'No,' she admitted. 'Can't you?'

He gave a short laugh. 'I wasn't expecting to.'

'Why not?'

His voice dipped. 'I suspect you know exactly why not. It's a somewhat *unusual* situation to be sharing a bed with an attractive woman and having to behave in such a chaste manner.'

Keira was glad of the darkness which hid her sudden flush of pleasure. Had the gorgeous and arrogant Matteo Valenti actually called her *attractive*? And was he really implying that he was having difficulty keeping his hands off her? Of course he might only be saying it to be polite—but he hadn't exactly been a model of politeness up until now, had he?

'I thought you said you didn't find me attractive?'

'That's what I was trying to convince myself.'

In the darkness, she gave a smile of pleasure. 'I could go downstairs and see if I could get us some more tea.'

'Please.' He groaned. 'No more tea.'

'Then I guess we'll have to resign ourselves to a sleepless night.' She plumped up her pillow and sighed as she collapsed back against it. 'Unless you've got a better suggestion?'

One Night With Consequences

When one night...leads to pregnancy!

When succumbing to a night of unbridled desire
it's impossible to think past the morning after!

But, with the sheets barely settled,
that little blue line appears on the pregnancy test and it
doesn't take long to realise that one night of white-hot
passion has turned into a lifetime of consequences!

Only one question remains:

How do you tell a man you've just met
that you're about to share more than just his bed?

Find out in:

Claiming His Christmas Consequence by Michelle Smart

The Guardian's Virgin Ward by Caitlin Crews

A Child Claimed by Gold by Rachael Thomas

The Consequence of His Vengeance by Jennie Lucas

Secrets of a Billionaire's Mistress by Sharon Kendrick

The Boss's Nine-Month Negotiation by Maya Blake

The Pregnant Kavakos Bride by Sharon Kendrick

A Ring for the Greek's Baby by Melanie Milburne

Engaged for Her Enemy's Heir by Kate Hewitt

The Virgin's Shock Baby by Heidi Rice

Look for more **One Night With Consequences** stories
coming soon!

THE ITALIAN'S CHRISTMAS SECRET

BY
SHARON KENDRICK

First Published in Great Britain 2017
By Mills & Boon, an imprint of HarperCollins*Publishers*
1 London Bridge Street, London, SE1 9GF

© 2017 Sharon Kendrick

ISBN: 978-0-263-07003-3

MIX
Paper from
responsible sources
FSC **FSC® C007454**
www.fsc.org

This book is produced from independently certified FSC paper
to ensure responsible forest management. For more information
visit www.harpercollins.co.uk/green.

Printed and bound in Great Britain
by CPI Group (UK) Ltd, Croydon, CR0 4YY

Sharon Kendrick once won a national writing competition by describing her ideal date: being flown to an exotic island by a gorgeous and powerful man. Little did she realise that she'd just wandered into her dream job! Today she writes for Mills & Boon, featuring often stubborn but always *to die for* heroes and the women who bring them to their knees. She believes that the best books are those you never want to end. Just like life...

Books by Sharon Kendrick

Mills & Boon Modern Romance

A Royal Vow of Convenience
The Ruthless Greek's Return
Christmas in Da Conti's Bed

One Night With Consequences

The Pregnant Kavakos Bride
Secrets of a Billionaire's Mistress
Crowned for the Prince's Heir
Carrying the Greek's Heir

Wedlocked!

The Sheikh's Bought Wife
The Billionaire's Defiant Acquisition

The Billionaire's Legacy

Di Sione's Virgin Mistress

The Bond of Billionaires

Claimed for Makarov's Baby
The Sheikh's Christmas Conquest

At His Service

The Housekeeper's Awakening

Visit the Author Profile page
at millsandboon.co.uk for more titles.

CHAPTER ONE

'MR VALENTI?'

The woman's soft voice filtered into Matteo's thoughts and he made no effort to hide his exasperation as he leaned back against the leather seat of the luxury car. He'd been thinking about his father. Wondering if he intended carrying out the blustering threat he'd made just before Matteo had left Rome—and if so, whether or not he could prevent it. He gave a heavy sigh, forcing himself to accept that the ties of blood went deeper than any others. They must do. He certainly wouldn't have tolerated so much from one person if they hadn't been related. But family were difficult to walk away from. Difficult to leave. He felt his heart clench. Unless, of course, they left you.

'Mr Valenti?' the soft voice repeated.

Matteo gave a small click of irritation and not just because he loathed people talking to him when it was clear he didn't want to be disturbed. It was more to do with the fact that this damned trip hadn't gone according to plan, and not just because he hadn't seen a single hotel he'd wanted to buy. It was as much to do with the small-boned female behind the steering wheel who was irritating the hell out of him.

'*Cos' hai detto?*' he demanded until the ensuing silence reminded him that the woman didn't speak Italian, that he was a long way from home—in fact, he was in the middle of the infernal English countryside with a woman driver.

He frowned. Having a woman chauffeur was a first for him and when he'd first seen her slender build and startled blue eyes, Matteo had been tempted to demand a replacement of the more burly male variety. Until he reminded himself that the last thing he needed was to be accused of sexual prejudice. His aristocratic nostrils flared as he glanced into the driver's mirror and met her eyes. 'What did you say?' he amended, in English.

The woman cleared her throat, her slim shoulders shifting slightly—though the ridiculous peaked cap she insisted on wearing over her shorn hair stayed firmly in place. 'I said that the weather seems to have taken a turn for the worse.'

Matteo turned his head to glance out of the window where the deepening dusk was almost obscured by the violent swirl of snowflakes. He'd been so caught up in his thoughts that he'd paid scant attention to the passing countryside but now he could see that the landscape was nothing but a bleached blur. He scowled. 'But we'll be able to get through?'

'I certainly hope so.'

'You hope so?' he echoed, his voice growing harder. 'What kind of an answer is that? You do realise that I have a flight all geared up and ready to go?'

'Yes, Mr Valenti. But it's a private jet and it will wait for you.'

'I am perfectly aware that it's a *private jet* since I happen to own it,' he bit out impatiently. 'But I'm due at a party in Rome tonight, and I don't intend being late.'

With a monumental effort Keira stifled a sigh and kept her eyes fixed on the snowy road ahead. She needed to act calm and stay calm because Matteo Valenti was the most important customer she'd ever driven, a fact her boss had drummed into her over and over again. Whatever happened, she mustn't show the nerves she'd been experiencing for the past few days—because driving a client of this calibre was a whole new experience for her. Being the only woman and the more junior driver on the payroll, she usually got different sorts of jobs. She collected urgent packages and delivered them, or picked up spoilt children from their prep school and returned them to their nanny in one of the many exclusive mansions which were dotted around London. But even mega-rich London customers paled into insignificance when you compared them with the wealth of Matteo Valenti.

Her boss had emphasised the fact that this was the first time the Italian billionaire had ever used their company and it was her duty to make sure he gave them plenty of repeat business. She thought it was great that such an influential tycoon had decided to give Luxury Limos his business, but she wasn't stupid. It was obvious he was only using them because he'd decided on the trip at the last minute—just as it was obvious she'd only been given the job because none of the other drivers were available, this close to Christmas. According to her boss, he was an important hotelier looking to buy a development site in England, to expand his growing empire of hotels. So far they had visited Kent, Sussex and Dorset—though they'd left the most far-flung destination of Devon until last, which wouldn't have been how *she* would have arranged it, especially not with the pre-holiday traffic being what it was. Still, she wasn't being employed to sort out his schedule for him—she was here to get him safely from A to B.

She stared straight ahead at the wild flurry of snowflakes. It was strange. She worked *with* men and *for* men and knew most of their foibles. She'd learnt that in order to be accepted it was better to act like one of the boys and not stand out. It was the reason she wore her hair short—though not the reason she'd cut it in the first place. It was why she didn't usually bother with make-up, or wearing the kind of clothes which invited a second look. The tomboy look suited her just fine, because if a man forgot you were there, he tended to relax—though unfortunately the same rule didn't seem to apply to Matteo Valenti. She'd never met a less relaxed individual.

But that wasn't the whole story, was it? She clutched the steering wheel tightly, unwilling to admit the real reason why she felt so self-conscious in his company. Because wasn't the truth that he had blown her away the moment they'd met, with the most potent brand of charisma she'd ever encountered? It was disturbing and exciting and scary all at the same time and it had never happened to her before—that thing of looking into someone's eyes and hearing a million violins start playing inside your head. She'd gazed into the darkest eyes she'd ever seen and felt as if she could drown in them. She'd found herself studying his thick black hair and wondering how it would feel to run her fingers through it. Failing that, having a half-friendly working relationship would have satisfied her, but that was never going to happen. Not with a man who was so abrupt, narrow-minded and *judgmental*.

She'd seen his expression when she'd been assigned to him, his black gaze raking over her with a look of incredulity he hadn't bothered to disguise. He'd actually had the nerve to ask whether she felt *confident* behind the wheel of such a powerful car and she had been tempted to coolly inform him that yes, she was, thank you very much. Just as she was confident about getting underneath the bonnet and taking the engine to pieces, should the need arise. And now he was snapping at her and making no attempt to hide his irritation—as if she had some kind of magical power over the weather conditions which had suddenly hit them from out of the blue!

She shot a nervous glance towards the heavy sky and felt another tug of anxiety as she met his hooded dark eyes in the driver's mirror.

'Where are we?' he demanded.

Keira glanced at the sat-nav. 'I think we're on Dartmoor.'

'You think?' he said sarcastically.

Keira licked her lips, glad he was now preoccupied with staring out of the window instead of glaring so intently at her. Glad he was ignorant of the sudden panicked pounding of her heart. 'The sat-nav lost its signal a couple of times.'

'But you didn't think to tell me that?'

She bit back her instinctive response that he was unlikely to be an expert on the more rural parts of the south-west since he'd told her he hardly ever visited England. Unless, of course, he was implying that his oozing masculinity was enough to compensate for a total lack of knowledge of the area.

'You were busy with a phone call at the time and I didn't like to interrupt,' she said. 'And you said...'

'I said what?'

She gave a little shrug. 'You mentioned that you'd like to travel back by the scenic route.'

Matteo frowned. Had he said that? It was true he'd been distracted by working out how he was going to deal with his father, but he didn't remember agreeing to some guided tour of an area he'd already decided wasn't for him, or his hotels. Hadn't it simply been a case of agreeing to her hesitant suggestion of an alternative route, when she'd told him that the motorways were likely to be busy with everyone travelling home for the Christmas holiday? In which case, surely she should have had the sense and the knowledge to anticipate something like this might happen.

'And this snowstorm seems to have come from out of nowhere,' she said.

With an effort Matteo controlled his temper, telling himself nothing would be achieved by snapping at her. He knew how erratic and *emotional* women could be—both in and out of the workplace—and had always

loathed overblown displays of emotion. She would probably burst into tears if he reprimanded her, followed
by an undignified scene while she blubbed into some
crumpled piece of tissue and then looked at him with
tragic, red-rimmed eyes. And scenes were something
he was at pains to avoid. He liked a life free of drama
and trauma. A life lived on his terms.

Briefly, he thought about Donatella waiting for him
at a party he wasn't going to be able to make. At the
disappointment in her green eyes when she realised
that several weeks of dating weren't going to end up
in a swish Roman hotel bedroom, as they'd planned.
His mouth hardened. He'd made her wait to have sex
with him and he could tell it had frustrated the hell out
of her. Well, she would just have to wait a little longer.

'Why don't you just get us there as safely as possible?' he suggested, zipping shut his briefcase. 'If I miss
the party, it won't be the end of the world—just so long
as I get home for Christmas in one piece. You can manage that, can't you?'

Keira nodded, but inside her heart was still racing
faster than it should have been considering her seden-
tary position behind the wheel. Because she was rapidly realising that they were in trouble. Real trouble.
Her windscreen wipers were going like crazy but no
sooner had they removed a thick mass of white flakes,
there were loads more their place. She'd never known
such awful visibility and found herself wondering why
she hadn't just risked the crowds and the traffic jams
and gone by the most direct route. Because she hadn't
wanted to risk a displeasure she suspected was never

very far from the surface with her billionaire client. Matteo Valenti wasn't the kind of person you could imagine sitting bumper to bumper on a road of stationary traffic while children in Santa hats pulled faces through the back windows. To be honest, she was surprised he didn't travel round by helicopter until he'd informed her that you got to see a lot more of the natural lie of the land from a car.

He seemed to have informed her about quite a lot of things. How he didn't like coffee from service stations and would rather go without food than eat something 'substandard'. How he preferred silence to the endless stream of Christmas songs on the car radio, though he didn't object when once she changed the station to some classical music, which she found strangely unsettling—particularly when a glance in the mirror showed her that he had closed his eyes and briefly parted his lips. Her heartbeat had felt *very* erratic after that particular episode.

Keira slowed down as they drove past a small house on which an illuminated Santa Claus was driving his sleigh above a garish sign proclaiming *Best Bed & Breakfast on Dartmoor!* The trouble was that she wasn't used to men like Matteo Valenti—she didn't imagine a lot of people were. She'd watched people's reactions whenever he emerged from the limousine to cast his eye over yet another dingy hotel which was up for sale. She'd witnessed women's gazes being drawn instinctively to his powerful physique. She'd watched their eyes widen—as if finding it hard to believe that one man could present such a perfect package, with those aristocratic features, hard jaw and sensual lips. But Keira had been up close to him for several days and she realised that, although he looked pretty perfect on the surface, there was a brooding quality underneath the surface which hinted at danger. And weren't a lot of women turned on by danger? As she clamped her fingers around the steering wheel, she wondered if that was the secret of his undeniable charisma.

But now wasn't the time to get preoccupied about Matteo Valenti, or even to contemplate the holidays which were fast approaching and which she was dreading. It was time to acknowledge that the snowstorm was getting heavier by the second and she was losing control of the big car. She could feel the tyres pushing against the weight of the accumulating drifts as the road took on a slight incline. She could feel sweat suddenly beading her brow as the heavy vehicle began to lose power and she realised that if she wasn't careful...

The car slid to a halt and Keira's knuckles whitened as she suddenly realised there were no distant tail lights in front of them. Or lights behind them. She glanced in the mirror as she turned off the ignition and forced herself to meet the furious black stare which was being directed at her from the back seat.

'What's going on?' he questioned, his tone sending a shiver rippling down Keira's spine.

'We've stopped,' she said, turning the key again and praying for them to start moving but the car stayed exactly where it was.

'I can see that for myself,' he snapped. 'The question is, *why* have we stopped?'

Keira gulped. He must have realised why. Did he want her to spell it out for him so he could shovel yet more blame on her? 'It's a heavy car and the snow is much thicker than I thought. We're on a slight hill, and...'

'And?'

Face facts, she told herself fiercely. You know how to do that. It's a difficult situation, but it's not the end of the world. She flicked the ignition and tried moving forward again but despite her silent prayers, the car stubbornly refused to budge. Her hands sliding reluctantly from the wheel, she turned round. 'We're stuck,' she admitted.

Matteo nodded, biting back the angry exclamation which was on the tip of his tongue, because he prided himself on being good in an emergency. God knew, there had been enough of those over the years to make him an expert in crisis management. Now was not the time to wonder why he hadn't followed his instincts and demanded a male driver who would have known what he was doing, instead of some slip of a girl who didn't look strong enough to control a pushbike, let alone a car this size. Recriminations could come later, he thought grimly—and they would. First and foremost they needed to get out of here—and to do that, they needed to keep their wits about them.

'Where exactly are we?' he said, speaking slowly as if to a very small child.

She swivelled her head to look at the sat-nav for several silent seconds before turning to meet his gaze again.

'The signal has cut out again. We're on the edge of Dartmoor.'

'How close to civilisation?'

'That's the trouble. We're not. We're miles from any-where.' He saw her teeth dig into her lower lip as if she were trying to draw blood from it. 'And there's no Wi-Fi connection,' she finished.

Matteo wanted to slam the flat of his hand against the snow-covered window but he sucked in an unsteady breath instead. He needed to take control.

'Move over,' he said roughly as he unclipped his seat belt.

She blinked those great big eyes at him. 'Move over where?'

'Onto the passenger seat,' he gritted out as he pushed open the car door to brace himself against a flurry of snowflakes. 'I'm taking over.'

He was pretty much covered in ice by the time he got into the car and slammed the door shut, and the bi-zarre thought which stuck in his mind was how deli-ciously warm the seat felt from where her bottom had been sitting.

Furious for allowing himself to be distracted by something so basic and inappropriate at a time like this, Matteo reached for the ignition key.

'You do know not to press down too hard on the accelerator, don't you?' she said nervously. 'Or you'll make the wheels spin.'

'I don't think I need any driving lessons from some-one as incompetent as you,' he retorted. He started the engine and tried moving forward. Nothing. He tried until he was forced to surrender to the inevitable, which deep down he'd known all along. They were well and truly stuck and the car wasn't going anywhere. He turned to the woman sitting beside him who was staring at him nervously from beneath her peaked cap.

'So. Bravo,' he said, his words steeped in an anger he could no longer contain. 'You've managed to get us stranded in one of the most inhospitable parts of the country on one of the most inhospitable nights of the year—just before Christmas. That's some feat!'

'I'm so sorry.'

'Saying sorry isn't going to help.'

'I'll probably get the sack,' she whispered.

'You will if I have anything to do with it—that's if you don't freeze to death first!' he snapped. 'If it were down to me, I would never have employed you in the first place. But the consequences to your career are the last thing on my mind right now. We need to start working out what we're going to do next.'

She reached into the glove compartment for her mobile phone but he wasn't surprised to see her grimace as she glanced down at the small screen. 'No signal,' she said, looking up.

'You don't say?' he said sarcastically, peering out of the window where the howling flakes showed no signs of abating. 'I'm guessing there's no nearby village?'

She shook her head. 'No. Well, we did pass a little B&B just a while back. You know, one of those places which offer bed and breakfast for the night.'

'I'm in the hotel trade,' he said silkily. 'And I'm perfectly aware of what a B&B is. How far was it?'

She shrugged. 'Less than a mile, I'd guess—though it wouldn't be easy to reach in this kind of conditions.'

'No kidding?' Matteo eyed the virtual white-out which was taking place outside the window and his heart thundered as he acknowledged the real danger of their situation. Because suddenly this was about more than just missing his flight or disappointing a woman who had been eager to make him her lover; this was about survival. Venturing outside in this kind of conditions would be challenging—and dangerous—and the alternative was to hunker down in the car for the night and wait for help to arrive tomorrow. Presumably she would have blankets in the boot and they could continue to run the heater. His lips curved into a grim smile. And wasn't the traditional method of generating heat to huddle two bodies together? But he gave the idea no more than a few seconds' thought before dismissing it—and not just because she didn't look as if she had enough flesh on her bones to provide any degree of comfort. No. To take the risk of staying put while the snow came down this fast would be nothing short of madness, for there was no guarantee anyone would find them in the morning.

He ran his gaze over her uniform of navy blue trousers and the sturdy jacket which matched her cap. The material curved over the faint swell of her breasts and brushed against her thighs and was hardly what you would call *practical*—certainly not appropriate to face the elements at their worst. He sighed. Which meant he would have to give her his overcoat and freeze to death himself. 'I don't suppose you have any warmer clothes with you?'

For a few seconds, she seemed to brighten. 'I've got an anorak in the boot.'

'An anorak?'

'It's a waterproof jacket. With a hood.' She removed her peaked chauffeur's cap and raked her fingers through her short dark hair and Matteo felt inexplicably irritated by the brief smile which had lightened her pale face.

Was she expecting praise for having had the foresight to pack a coat? he wondered acidly.

'Just get it and put it on,' he bit out. 'And then let's get the hell out of here.'

CHAPTER TWO

KEIRA HAD TO work hard to keep up with Matteo as he battled his way through the deep snow because his powerful body moved much faster than hers, despite the fact that he'd insisted on bringing his suitcase with him. Thick, icy flakes were flying into her eyes and mouth and at times she wondered if she was imagining the small lighted building in the distance—like some bizarre, winter version of an oasis.

Despite putting on the big pair of leather gloves he'd insisted she borrow, her fingers felt like sticks of ice and she gave a little cry of relief when at last they reached the little house. Thank heavens she *hadn't* imagined it because she didn't like to think about Matteo Valenti's reaction if she'd brought him here on a wild goose chase. He might have insisted on her borrowing his gloves, but even that had been done with a terse impatience. She saw his unsmiling look as he kicked a pile of snow away from the wooden gate and pushed it open, and she stumbled after him up the path to stand beneath the flashing red and gold lights of the illuminated sign overhead. She was shivering with cold by the time he'd jammed his finger on the doorbell and they heard some tinkly little tune playing in the distance.

'Wh-what if…wh-what if nobody's in?' she questioned from between teeth which wouldn't seem to stop chattering.

'The light's on,' he said impatiently. 'Of course somebody's in.'

'They m-might have gone away for Christmas and left the lights on a timer to deter burglars.'

'You really think burglars are going to be enticed by a place like *this*?' he demanded.

But their bad-tempered interchange was brought to a swift halt by the sound of a lumbering movement from within the house and the door was pulled open by a plump, middle-aged woman wearing a flowery apron which was smeared with flour.

'Well, bless my soul!' she said, opening the door wider as she peered out into the gloom. 'You're not carol singers, are you?'

'We are not,' answered Matteo grimly. 'I'm afraid our car has got snowed in a little way down the road.'

'Oh, you poor things! What a night to be outside! Come in, come in!'

Keira felt like bursting into tears of gratitude as Matteo's palm positioned itself in the small of her back and propelled her inside the bright little hallway. During the seemingly endless journey here, she'd been convinced they weren't going to make it, and that their two frozen figures would be discovered the next day, or the day after that. And hadn't she been unable to stop herself from wondering whether anyone would have actually *cared* if she died?

But now they were standing dripping in a small hallway which had boughs of holly and strands of glittery tinsel draped absolutely everywhere. A green plastic tree was decked with flashing rainbow lights and from a central light hung a huge bunch of mistletoe. Keira's eyes were drawn in fascination to the row of small, fluffy snowmen waddling in a perfectly symmetrical line along a shelf—her attention only distracted by the realisation that puddles of water were growing on the stone tiles beneath their feet. Years of being told to respect property—especially when it *wasn't your own*—made Keira concentrate on the mess they were making, rather than the glaringly obvious fact that she and her bad-tempered Italian client were gate-crashing someone else's Christmas.

'Oh, my goodness—look at the floor!' she said, aware of the faint look of incredulity which Matteo Valenti was slanting in her direction. 'We're ruining your floor.'

'Don't you worry about that, my dear,' said the woman in her warm West Country accent. 'We get walkers coming in here all the time—that'll soon clean up.'

'We'd like to use your phone if that's okay,' said Matteo, and Keira watched as the woman looked at him, her mouth opening and closing comically as if she'd only just realised that she had six feet three inches of brooding masculine gorgeousness in her house, with melting snow sliding down over his black cashmere coat.

'And why would you want to do that, dear?' questioned the woman mildly.

Matteo did his best not to flinch at the overfamiliar response, even though he despised endearments from complete strangers. Actually, he despised endearments generally. Didn't they say that you always mistrusted what you weren't used to? Suppressing a frustrated flicker of anger at having found himself in this intolerable situation, he decided he needed to own it. Better to calmly spell out their needs, since his driver seemed incapable of doing anything with any degree of competence. 'Our car has become imbedded in the snow just down the road a little,' he said, directing an accusing glare at the woman who was currently pulling off her bulky waterproof jacket and shaking her short dark hair. 'We should never have taken this route, given the weather. However, what's done is done and we can't do anything about that now. We just need to get out of here, as quickly as possible, and I'd like to arrange that immediately.'

The woman nodded, her bright smile remaining unfaltering. 'I don't think that's going to be possible, dear. You won't get a rescue truck to dig you out—not tonight. Why, nothing's going to get through—not in these conditions!'

It was the confirmation of his worst fears and although Matteo was tempted to vent his rage, he was aware it would serve no useful purpose—as well as insulting the woman who'd been kind enough to open her house to them. And she was right. Who could possibly get to them tonight—in weather like this? He needed to face facts and accept that he was stuck here, in the middle of nowhere—with his incompetent driver in tow. A driver who was staring at him with eyes which suddenly looked very dark in her pale face. He frowned.

Of all the females in the world to be stranded with—it had to be someone like her! Once again his thoughts drifted to the luxurious party he would be missing, but he dismissed them as he drew in a deep breath and forced himself to say the unimaginable. 'Then it looks as if we're going to have to stay here. I assume you have rooms for hire?'

The woman's wide smile slipped. 'In December? Not likely! All my rooms are fully booked,' she added proudly. 'I get repeat trade all through the year, but especially at this time of year. People love a romantic Christmas on Dartmoor!'

'But we need somewhere to stay,' butted in Keira suddenly. 'Just until morning. Hopefully the snow will have stopped by then and we can get on our way in the morning.'

The woman nodded, her gaze running over Keira's pale cheeks as she took the anorak from her and hung it on a hook. 'Well, I'm hardly going to turn you out on a night like this, am I? Especially not at this time of the year—I'm sure we can find you room at the inn! I can put you in my daughter's old bedroom at the back of the house. That's the only space I have available. But the dining room is completely booked out and so I'm afraid I can't offer you dinner.'

'The meal doesn't matter,' put in Matteo quickly.

'Maybe if you could send something to the room when you have a moment?'

Keira felt numb as they were shown up some rickety stairs at the back of the house, and she remained numb as the landlady—who informed them that her name was Mary—opened the door with a flourish.

'You should be comfortable enough in here,' she said. 'The bathroom is just along the corridor though there's not much water left, and if you want a bath, you'll have to share. I'll just go downstairs and put the kettle on. Make yourselves at home.'

Mary shut the door behind her and Keira's heart started racing as she realised that she was alone in a claustrophobic space with Matteo Valenti. Make themselves at home? How on earth were they going to do that in a room this size with *only one bed*?

She shivered. 'Why didn't you tell her that we didn't want to share?'

He shot her an impatient look. 'We are two people and she has one room. You do the math. What alternative did I have?'

Keira could see his point. Mary couldn't magic up another bedroom from out of nowhere, could she? She looked around. It was one of those rooms which wasn't really big enough for the furniture it contained. It was too small for a double bed, but a double bed had been crammed into it nonetheless, and it dominated the room with its homemade patchwork quilt and faded pillow cases on which you could just about make out some Disney characters, one of which just happened to be Cinderella.

There were no signs of Christmas in here but on every available surface seemed to be a photo. Photos of someone who was recognisably Mary, looking much younger and holding a series of babies, then toddlers, right through gangly teenagers until the inevitable stiff wedding photos—and then yet more babies. Keira licked her lips. It was a life played out in stills. A simple life, probably—and a happy life, judging by the smile which was never far from Mary's face. Keira was used to cramped and cluttered spaces but she wasn't used to somewhere feeling homely—and she could do absolutely nothing about the fierce pang of something which felt like envy, which clutched at her heart like a vice.

She lifted her eyes to meet Matteo's flat gaze. 'I'm sorry,' she said.

'Spare me the platitudes,' he snapped, pulling out the mobile phone from the pocket of his trousers and staring at it with a barely concealed lack of hope. 'No signal. Of course there isn't. And no Wi-Fi either.'

'She said you could use the landline any time.'

'I know she did. I'll call my assistant once I've removed some of these wet clothes.' He loosened his tie before tugging it off and throwing it over the back of a nearby chair, where it dangled like some precious spiral of gunmetal. His mouth hardened with an expression of disbelief as he looked around. *'Per amor del cielo!* Who even uses places like this? We don't even have our own bathroom.'

'Mary told us we could use the one along the corridor.'

'She also told us that we'd need to share a bath because there wasn't enough hot water!' he flared. '*Sharing a bath? Not enough hot water?* Which century are we supposed to be living in?'

Keira shrugged her shoulders awkwardly, suspecting that Matteo Valenti wasn't used to the vagaries of small-town English landladies, or the kind of places where ordinary people stayed. Of course he wasn't. According to her boss, he owned luxury hotels all over his own country—he even had some scattered over America, as well as some in Barbados and Hawaii. What would he know about having to traipse along a chilly corridor to a bathroom which, like the rest of the house, obviously hadn't been modernised in decades?

'It's an English eccentricity. Part of the place's charm,' she added lamely.

'Charm I can do without,' he responded acidly. 'Good plumbing trumps charm every time.'

She wondered if he was deliberately ignoring something even more disturbing than the bathroom facilities…or maybe she was just being super-sensitive about it, given her uneasy history. Awkwardly she raked her fingers through her spiky hair, wondering what it was which marked her out from other women. Why was it that on the only two occasions she'd shared a bed with a man, one had been passed out drunk—while the other was looking at her with nothing but irritation in his hard black eyes?

He was nodding his head, as if she had spoken out loud. 'I know,' he said grimly. 'It's my idea of a nightmare, too. Sharing a too-small bed with an employee wasn't top of my Christmas wish list.'

Don't react, Keira told herself fiercely. And don't take it personally. Act with indifference and don't make out like it's a big deal.

'I expect we'll survive,' she said coolly, then began to rub at her arms through the thin jacket as she started to shiver.

He ran a speculative gaze over her and an unexpected note of consideration crept into his voice. 'You're cold,' he said, his eyes lingering on her thighs just a fraction too long. 'And your trousers are soaking.'

'You don't say?' she said, her voice rising a little defensively, because she'd never been very good at dealing with unsolicited kindness.

'Don't you have anything else you can wear?' he persisted.

Embarrassment made her even more defensive and Keira glared at him, aware of the heat now staining her cheeks. 'Yes, of course I do. I always make sure I carry an entire change of clothes with me whenever I embark on a drive from London to Devon,' she said. 'It's what every driver does.'

'Why don't you skip the sarcasm?' he suggested. 'And go and take a hot bath? You can borrow something of mine.'

Keira looked at him suspiciously, taken aback by the offer and not quite sure if he meant it. Without his cashmere coat he stood resplendent in a dark charcoal suit which, even to her untutored eye, she could tell was made-to-measure. It must have been—because surely your average suit didn't cater for men with shoulders as broad as his, or legs that long. What on earth could Matteo Valenti have in his suitcase which would fit *her*? 'You carry women's clothes around with you, do you?'

An unexpected smile lifted the corners of his mouth and the corresponding race of Keira's heart made her hope he wasn't going to do a lot of smiling.

'Funnily enough, no,' he said drily, unzipping the leather case. 'But I have a sweater you can use. And a soap bag. Here. Go on. Take it.'

He was removing the items from his case and handing them to her and Keira was overcome by a sudden gratitude. 'Th-thanks. You're very kind—'

'*Basta!* Spare me the stumbling appreciation. I'm not doing it out of any sense of *kindness*.' His mouth hardened. 'This day has already been a disaster—I don't want to add to the misery by having you catch pneumonia and finding myself with a wrongful death suit on my hands.'

'Well, I'll do my best not to get sick then,' she bit back. 'I'd hate to inconvenience you any more than I already have done!'

Her fingers digging into his sweater, Keira marched from the room to the bathroom along the corridor, trying to dampen down her rising feelings of anger. He really was the most hateful person she'd ever met and she was going to have to endure a whole night with him.

Hanging his sweater on the back of the door, she quickly assessed the facilities on offer and for the first time that day, she smiled. Good thing *she* was used to basics. To her the avocado-coloured sink and bath were nothing out of the ordinary, though she shuddered to think how Mr Cynical was going to cope. When she'd been growing up, she and her mother had lived in places with far worse plumbing than this. In fact, this rather tatty bathroom felt almost *nostalgic*. A throwback to tougher times, yes, but at least it had been one of those rare times when she'd known emotional security, before Mum had died.

Clambering into the tiny bath, she directed the leaking shower attachment over her head and sluiced herself with tepid water before lathering on some of Matteo's amazing soap. And then the strangest thing started happening. Beneath her massaging fingers she could feel her nipples begin to harden into tight little nubs and for a moment she closed her eyes as she imagined her powerful client touching her there, before pulling her hands away in horror. What on earth was *wrong* with her?

Leaving the plug in situ and climbing out of the tub, she furiously rubbed herself dry. Wasn't the situation bad enough without her fantasising about a man who was probably going to make sure she got fired as soon as they reached civilisation?

She put on her bra, turned her knickers inside out and slithered Matteo's grey sweater over her head. It was warm and very soft—it was just unfortunate that it only came to mid-thigh, no matter how hard she tugged at the hem. She stared into the mirror. And the problem with that was, what? Was she really naïve enough to think that the Italian tycoon would even *notice* what she was wearing? Why, judging from his attitude towards her up until now, she could probably waltz back in there completely naked and he wouldn't even bat those devastatingly dark eyelashes.

But about that Keira was wrong—just as she'd been wrong in making the detour via Dartmoor—because when she walked back into the bedroom Matteo Valenti turned around from where he had been standing gazing out of the window and, just like the weather outside, his face froze. It was extraordinary to witness, that unmistakable double take when he saw her, something which never normally happened when Keira walked into a room. His eyes narrowed and grew smoky and something in the atmosphere seemed to subtly shift, and change. She wasn't used to it, but she wasn't going to deny that it made her skin grow warm with pleasure. Unless, of course, she was totally misreading the situation. It wouldn't be the first time, would it?

'Is everything okay?' she asked uncertainly.

Matteo nodded in response, aware that a pulse had begun to hammer at his temple. He'd just finished a telephone conversation with his assistant and as a consequence he'd been miles away, staring out of the window at the desolate countryside and having the peculiar sensation of realising that nobody could get hold of him—a sensation which had brought with it a surprising wave of peace. He had watched his driver scuttle off towards the bathroom in her unflattering navy trouser suit, only now she had returned and…

He stared and swallowed down the sudden lump which had risen in his throat. It was inexplicable. What the hell had she done to herself?

Her short, dark hair was still drying and the heat

of the shower must have been responsible for the rosy flush of her cheeks, against which her sapphire eyes looked huge and glittery. But it was his sweater which was responsible for inflicting a sudden sexual awakening he would have preferred to avoid. A plain cashmere sweater which looked like a completely different garment when worn by her. She was so small and petite that it pretty much swamped her, but it hinted at the narrow-hipped body beneath and the most perfect pair of legs he had ever seen. She looked...

He shook his head slightly. She looked *sexy,* he thought resentfully as lust arrowed straight to his groin, where it hardened and stayed. She looked as if she wanted him to lay her down on the bed and start kissing her. As if she were tantalising him with the question of whether or not she was wearing any panties. He felt he was in a schoolboy's fantasy, tempted to ask her to bend down to pick up some imaginary object from the carpet so he could see for himself if her bottom was bare. And then he glared because the situation was bad enough without having to endure countless hours of frustration, daydreaming about a woman he couldn't have—even if he was the kind of man to indulge in a one-night stand, which he most emphatically wasn't.

'*Sì*, everything is wonderful. *Fantastico,*' he added sarcastically. 'I've just made a phone call to my assistant and asked her to make my apologies for tonight's party. She asked if I was doing something nice instead and I told her that no, I was not. In fact, I was stuck on a snowy moor in the middle of nowhere.'

'I've left you some hot water,' she said stiffly, deciding to ignore his rant.

'How will I be able to contain my excitement?' he returned as he picked up the clothes he had selected from his case and slammed his way out of the room.

But he'd calmed down a little by the time he returned, dressed down in jeans and a sweater, to find her stirring a pot of tea which jostled for space on a tray containing sandwiches and mince pies. She turned her face towards him with a questioning look.

'Are you hungry?' she said.

It was difficult to return her gaze when all he wanted to do was focus on her legs and that still tantalising question of what she was or wasn't wearing underneath his sweater. Matteo shrugged. 'I guess.'

'Would you like a sandwich?'

'How can I refuse?'

'It's very kind of Mary to have gone to the trouble of making us some, especially when she's trying to cook a big turkey dinner for eight people,' she admonished quietly. 'The least we can do is be grateful.'

'I suppose so.'

Keira tried to maintain her polite smile as she handed him a cup of tea and a cheese sandwich, telling herself that nothing would be gained by being rude herself. In fact, it would only make matters worse if they started sparring. She was the one in the wrong and the one whose job was on the line. If she kept answering him back, who was to say he wouldn't ring up her boss and subject him to a blistering tirade about her incompetence? If she kept him sweet, mightn't he be persuaded not to make a big deal out of the situation, maybe even to forget it had ever happened and put it down to experience? She needed this job because she loved it and things to love in Keira's life happened too rarely for her to want to give them up without a fight.

She noticed that he said nothing as he ate, his expression suggesting he was merely fuelling his impressive body rather than enjoying what was on offer—but Keira's hunger had completely deserted her and that was a first. She normally had a healthy appetite, which often surprised people who commented on her tiny frame. But not today. Today food was the last thing on her mind. She broke off the rim of one of the mince pies and forced herself to chew on it and the sugar gave her a sudden rush, but all she could think about was how on earth they were going to get through the hours ahead, when there wasn't even a radio in the room— let alone a TV. She watched the way the lamplight fell on her client's face—the hardness of his features contrasting with the sensual curve of his lips—and found herself wondering what it might be like to be kissed by a man like him.

Stop it, she urged herself furiously. Just *stop* it. You couldn't even maintain the interest of that trainee mechanic you dated in the workshop—do you really fancy your chances with the Italian billionaire?

A note of desperation tinged her voice as she struggled to think of something they could do which might distract her from all that brooding masculinity. 'Shall I go downstairs and see if Mary has any board games we could play?'

He put his empty cup down and his eyes narrowed. 'Excuse me?'

'You know.' She shrugged her shoulders helplessly. 'Cards, or Scrabble or Monopoly. Something,' she added. 'Because we can't just spend the whole evening staring at each other and dreading the night ahead, can we?'

He raised his dark eyebrows. 'You're dreading the night ahead, are you, Keira?'

A shimmer of amusement had deepened his voice and Keira realised that, not only was it the first time he'd actually used her name, but that he'd said it as no one had ever said it before. She could feel colour flushing over her cheekbones and knew she had to stop coming over as some kind of unworldly idiot. 'Well, aren't you?' she challenged. 'Don't tell me your heart didn't sink when you realised we'd have to spend the night here.'

Matteo considered her question. Up until a few moments ago he might have agreed with her, but there was something about the girl with the spiky black hair which was making him reconsider his original assessment. It was, he thought, a novel situation and he was a man whose appetites had been jaded enough over the years to be entertained by the novel. And Keira whatever-her-name-was certainly wasn't your average woman. She wasn't behaving as most women would have done in the circumstances. She had suggested playing a game as if she actually meant it, without any purring emphasis on the word *playing*, leaving him in no doubt how she intended the 'game' to progress—with him thrusting into her eager body. People called him arrogant, but he preferred to think of himself as a realist. He'd never been guilty of under-assessing his own attributes—and one of those was his ability to make the opposite sex melt, without even trying.

He focussed his gaze on her, mildly amused by the competitive look in her eyes which suggested that her question had been genuine. 'Sure,' he said. 'Let's play games.'

Picking up the tray, she went downstairs, reappearing after a little while with a stack of board games, along with a bottle of red wine and two glasses.

'There's no need to be snobby about the vintage,' she said, noticing his expression as he frowningly assessed the label on the bottle. 'It was very sweet of Mary to offer us a festive drink and I'm having a glass even if you aren't. I'm not driving anywhere tonight and I don't want to offend her, not when she's been so kind.'

Feeling surprisingly chastened, Matteo took the bottle and opened it, pouring them each a glass and forcing himself to drink most of his in a single draught as he lowered himself into the most uncomfortable chair he'd ever sat in.

'Ready?' she questioned as she sat cross-legged on the bed, with a blanket placed discreetly over her thighs as she faced him.

'I guess,' he growled.

They played Monopoly, which naturally he won—but then, he'd spent all his adult life trading property and had learnt early that there was no commodity more precious than land. But he was surprised when she suggested a quick game of poker and even more surprised by her skill with the cards.

Matteo wondered afterwards if he'd been distracted by knowing her legs were bare beneath the blanket. Or if he'd just spent too long gazing at her curling black lashes, which remarkably didn't carry a trace of mascara. Because wasn't the truth that he was finding his pocket-sized driver more fascinating with every moment which passed? She was certainly managing to keep her face poker-straight as she gazed at her cards and inexplicably he found himself longing to kiss those unsmiling lips.

He swallowed. Was she aware that her coolness towards him was fanning a sexual awareness which was growing fiercer by the second? He didn't know—all he *did* know was that by the time they'd drunk most of the bottle of wine, she had beaten him hands-down and it was an unfamiliar experience.

He narrowed his eyes. 'Who taught you to play like that?'

She shrugged. 'Before I became a driver, I worked as a car mechanic—mostly with men,' she added airily. 'And they liked to play cards when the workshop was quiet.'

'You worked as a *car mechanic*?'

'You sound surprised.'

'I am surprised. You don't look strong enough to take a car to pieces.'

'Appearances can be deceptive.'

'They certainly can.' He picked up the bottle and emptied out the last of the wine, noticing her fingers

tremble as he handed her the glass. She must be feeling it too, he thought grimly—that almost tangible buzz
of *electricity* when his hand brushed against hers. He
crossed one leg over the other to hide the hard throb of
his erection as he tried—and failed—to think of something which didn't involve his lips and her body.

'Mr Valenti,' she said suddenly.

'Matteo,' he instructed silkily. 'I thought we agreed
we should be on first-name terms, given the somewhat
unusual circumstances.'

'Yes, we did, but I…

Keira's words tailed away as he fixed her with a
questioning look, not quite sure how to express her
thoughts. The alcohol had made her feel more daring
than usual—something which she'd fully exploited during that game of cards. She'd known it probably wasn't
the most sensible thing to defeat Matteo Valenti and yet
something had made her want to show him she wasn't
as useless as he seemed to think she was. But she was
now aware of her bravado slipping away. Just as she
was aware of the tension which had been building in
the cramped bedroom ever since she'd emerged from
the bathroom.

Her breasts were aching and her inside-out panties
were wet. Did he realise that? Perhaps he was used to
women reacting that way around him but she wasn't
one of those women. She'd been called frigid by men
before, when really she'd been scared—scared of doing
what her mother had always warned her against. But it
had never been a problem before, because close contact
with the opposite sex had always left her cold and the

one time she'd ended up in bed with a man he had been snoring in a drunken stupor almost before his head had hit the pillow. So how was Matteo managing to make her feel like this—as if every pore were screaming for him to touch her?

She swallowed. 'We haven't discussed what we're going to do about sleeping arrangements.'

'What did you have in mind?'

'Well, it looks as if we've got to share a bed—so obviously we've got to come to some sort of compromise.' She drew a deep breath. 'And I was thinking we might sleep top and tail.'

'Top and tail?' he repeated.

'You know.'

'Obviously I don't,' he said impatiently. 'Or I wouldn't have asked.'

Awkwardly, she wriggled her shoulders. 'It's easy. I sleep with my head at one end of the bed and you sleep with yours at the other. We used to do it when I was in the Girl Guides. Sometimes people even put pillows between them, so they can keep to their side and there's no encroaching on the other person's space.' She forged on but it wasn't easy when he was staring at her with a growing look of incredulity. 'Unless you're prepared to spend the night in that armchair?'

Matteo became aware of the hardness of the over-stuffed seat which made him feel as if he were sitting on spirals of iron. 'You honestly think I'm going to spend the night sitting in this damned chair?'

She looked at him uncertainly. 'You want *me* to take the chair?'

'And keep me awake all night while you shift around trying to get comfortable? No. I do not. I'll tell you exactly what's going to happen, *cara mia*. We're going to share that bed as the nice lady suggested. But don't worry, I will break the habit of a lifetime by not sleeping naked and you can keep the sweater on. *Capisci?* And you can rest assured that you'll be safe from my intentions because I don't find you in the least bit attractive.'

Which wasn't exactly true—but why make a grim situation even worse than it already was?

He stood up and as he began to undo the belt of his trousers, he saw her lips fall open. 'Better close those big blue eyes,' he suggested silkily, a flicker of amusement curving his lips as he watched all the colour drain from her cheeks. 'At least until I'm safely underneath the covers.'

CHAPTER THREE

KEIRA LAY IN the darkness nudging her tongue over lips which felt as dry as if she'd been running a marathon. She'd tried everything. Breathing deeply. Counting backwards from a thousand. Relaxing her muscles from the toes up. But up until now nothing had worked and all she could think about was the man in bed beside her. *Matteo Valenti. In bed beside her.* She had to keep silently repeating it to herself to remind herself of the sheer impossibility of the situation—as well as the undeniable temptation which was fizzing over her.

Sheer animal warmth radiated from his powerful frame, making her want to squirm with an odd kind of frustration. She kept wanting to fidget but she forced herself to lie as still as possible, terrified of waking him up. She kept telling herself that she'd been up since six that morning and should be exhausted, but the more she reached out for sleep, the more it eluded her.

Was it because that unwilling glimpse of his body as he was about to climb into bed had reinforced all the fantasies she'd been trying not to have? And yes, he'd covered up with a T-shirt and a pair of silky boxers—

but they did nothing to detract from his hard-packed abdomen and hair-roughened legs. Each time she closed her eyes she could picture all that hard, honed muscle and a wave of hunger shivered over her body, leaving her almost breathless with desire.

The sounds coming from downstairs didn't help. The dinner which Mary had mentioned was in full flow and bothering her in ways she'd prefer not to think about. She could hear squeals of excitement above the chatter and, later, the heartbreaking strains of children's voices as they started singing carols. She could picture them all by a roaring log fire with red candles burning on the mantle above, just like on the front of a Christmas card, and Keira felt a wave of wistfulness overwhelm her because she'd never had that.

'Can't sleep?' The Italian's silky voice penetrated her spinning thoughts and she could tell from the shifting weight on the mattress that Matteo Valenti had turned his head to talk to her.

Keira swallowed. Should she pretend to be asleep? But what would be the point of that? She suspected he would see through her ruse immediately—and wasn't it a bit of a relief not to have to keep still any more? 'No,' she admitted. 'Can't you?'

He gave a short laugh. 'I wasn't expecting to.'

'Why not?'

His voice dipped. 'I suspect you know exactly why not. It's a somewhat *unusual* situation to be sharing a bed with an attractive woman and having to behave in such a chaste manner.'

Keira was glad of the darkness which hid her sudden

flush of pleasure. Had the gorgeous and arrogant Matteo Valenti actually called her *attractive*? And was he really implying that he was having difficulty keeping his hands off her? Of course, he might only be saying it to be polite—but he hadn't exactly been the model of politeness up until now, had he?

'I thought you said you didn't find me attractive.'

'That's what I was trying to convince myself.'

In the darkness, she gave a smile of pleasure. 'I could go downstairs and see if I could get us some more tea.'

'Please.' He groaned. 'No more tea.'

'Then I guess we'll have to resign ourselves to a sleepless night.' She plumped up her pillow and sighed as she collapsed back against it. 'Unless you've got a better suggestion?'

Matteo gave a frustrated smile because her question sounded genuine. She wasn't asking it in such a way which demanded he lean over and give her the answer with his lips. Just as she wasn't accidentally brushing one of those pretty little legs against his and tantalising him with her touch. He swallowed. Not that her virtuous attitude made any difference because he'd been hard from the moment he'd first slipped beneath the covers, and he was rock-hard now. Hard for a woman with terrible hair whose incompetence was responsible for him being marooned in this hellhole in the first place! A different kind of frustration washed over him as the lumpy mattress dug into his back until he reminded himself that apportioning blame would serve little purpose.

'I guess we could talk,' he said.

'What about?'

'What do women like best to talk about?' he questioned sardonically. 'You could tell me something about yourself.'

'And what good will that do?'

'Probably send me off to sleep,' he admitted.

He could hear her give a little snort of laughter. 'You do say some outrageous things, Mr Valenti.'

'Guilty. And I thought we agreed on Matteo—at least while we're in bed together.' He smiled as he heard her muffled gasp of outrage. 'Tell me how you plan to spend Christmas—isn't that what everyone asks at this time of year?'

Beneath the duvet, Keira flexed and unflexed her fingers, thinking that of all the questions he *could* have asked, that was the one she least felt like answering. Why hadn't he asked her about cars so she could have dazzled him with her mechanical knowledge? Or told him about her pipedream of one day being able to restore beautiful vintage cars, even though realistically that was never going to happen. 'With my aunt and my cousin, Shelley,' she said grudgingly.

'But you're not looking forward to it?'

'Is it that obvious?'

'I'm afraid it is. Your voice lacked a certain…enthusiasm.'

She thought that was a very diplomatic way of putting it. 'No, I'm not.'

'So why not spend Christmas somewhere else?'

Keira sighed. In the darkness it was all too easy to forget the veneer of nonchalance she always adopted when people asked questions about her personal life.

She kept facts to a minimum because it was easier that way. If you made it clear you didn't want to talk about something, then eventually people stopped asking.

But Matteo was different. She wasn't ever going to see him again after tomorrow. And wasn't it good to be able to say what she felt for once, instead of what she knew people expected to hear? She knew she was lucky her aunt had taken her in when that drunken joy-rider had mown down her mother on her way home from work, carrying the toy dog she'd bought for her daughter's birthday. Lucky she hadn't had to go into a foster home or some scary institution. But knowing something didn't always change the way you felt inside. And it didn't change the reality of being made to feel like an imposition. Of constantly having to be grateful for having been given a home, when it was clear you weren't really wanted. Trying to ignore all the snide little barbs because Keira had been better looking than her cousin Shelley. It had been the reason she'd cut off all her hair one day and kept it short. Anything for a quiet life. 'Because Christmas is a time for families and they're the only one I have,' she said.

'You don't have parents?'

'No.' And then, because he seemed to have left a gap for her to fill, she found herself doing exactly that. 'I didn't know my father and my aunt brought me up after my mother died, so I owe her a lot.'

'But you don't like her?'

'I didn't say that.'

'You didn't have to. It isn't a crime to admit it. You

don't have to like someone, just because they were kind to you, Keira, even if they're a relative.'

'She did her best and it can't have been easy. There wasn't a lot of money sloshing around,' she said. 'And now my uncle has died, there's only the two of them and I think she's lonely, in a funny kind of way. So I shall be sitting round a table with her and my cousin, pulling Christmas crackers and pretending to enjoy dry turkey. Just like most people, I guess.'

There was a pause so long that for a moment Keira wondered if he *had* fallen asleep, so that when he spoke again it startled her.

'So what *would* you do over Christmas?' he questioned softly. 'If money were no object and you didn't have to spend time with your aunt?'

Keira pulled the duvet up to her chin. 'How much money are we talking about? Enough to charter a private jet and fly to the Caribbean?'

'If that's what turns you on.'

'Not particularly.' Keira looked at the faint gleam of a photo frame glowing in the darkness on the other side of the room. It was a long time since she'd played make-believe. A long time since she'd dared. 'I'd book myself into the most luxurious hotel I could find,' she said slowly, 'and I'd watch TV. You know, one of those TVs which are big enough to fill a wall—big as a cinema screen. I've never had a TV in the bedroom before and it would be showing every cheesy Christmas film ever made. So I'd lie there and order up ice cream and popcorn and eat myself stupid and try not to blub too much.'

Beneath the thin duvet, Matteo's body tensed and not just because of the wistfulness in her voice. It had been a long time since he'd received such an uncomplicated answer from anyone. And wasn't her simple candour refreshing? As refreshing as her lean young body and eyes which were *profundo blu* if you looked at them closely—the colour of the deep, dark sea. The beat of his heart had accelerated and he felt the renewed throb of an erection, heavy against his belly. And suddenly the darkness represented danger because it was cloaking him with anonymity. Making him forget who he was and who she was. Tempting him with things he shouldn't even be thinking about. Because without light they were simply two bodies lying side by side, at the mercy of their senses—and right then his senses were going into overdrive.

Reaching out his arm, he snapped on the light, so that the small bedroom was flooded with a soft glow, and Keira lay there with the duvet right up to her chin, blinking her eyes at him.

'What did you do that for?'

'Because I'm finding the darkness…distracting.'

'I don't understand.'

He raised his eyebrows. 'Don't you?'

There was a pause. Matteo could see wariness in her eyes as she shook her head, but he could see the flicker of something else, something which made his heart pound even harder. Fraternising with the workforce was a bad idea—everyone knew that. But knowing something didn't always change the way you felt. It didn't stop your body from becoming so tight with lust that it felt like a taut bow, just before the arrow was fired.

No,' she said at last. 'I don't.'

'I think I'd better go and sleep in that damned armchair after all,' he said. 'Because if I stay here any longer I'm going to start kissing you.'

Keira met his mocking black gaze in astonishment. Had Matteo Valenti just said he wanted to *kiss* her? For a moment she just lay there, revelling in the sensation of being the object of attraction to such a gorgeous man, while common sense pitched a fierce battle with her senses.

She realised that despite talking about the armchair he hadn't moved and that an unspoken question seemed to be hovering in the air. Somewhere in a distant part of the house she heard a clock chiming and, though it wasn't midnight, it felt like the witching hour. As if magic could happen if she only let it. If she listened to what she wanted rather than the voice of caution which had been a constant presence in her life ever since she could remember. She'd learnt the hard way what happened to women who fell for the wrong kind of man— and Matteo Valenti had *wrong* written on every pore of his body. He was dangerous and sexy and he was a billionaire who was way out of her league. Shouldn't she be turning away from him and telling him yes, to please take the armchair?

Yet she wasn't doing any of those things. Instead of her eyes closing, the tip of her tongue was sliding over her bottom lip and she was finding it impossible to drag her gaze away from him. She could feel a molten heat low in her belly, which was making her ache in a way which was shockingly exciting. She thought about the holidays ahead. The stilted Christmas lunch with her aunt beaming at Shelley and talking proudly of her daughter's job as a beautician, while wondering how her only niece had ended up as a car mechanic.

Briefly Keira closed her eyes. She'd spent her whole life trying to be good and where had it got her? You didn't get medals for being good. She'd made the best of her dyslexia and capitalised on the fact that she was talented with her hands and could take engines apart, then put them back together. She'd found a job in a man's world which was just about making ends meet, but she'd never had a long-term relationship. She'd never even had sex—and if she wasn't careful she might end up old and wistful, remembering a snowy night on Dartmoor when Matteo Valenti had wanted to kiss her.

She stared at him. 'Go on, then,' she whispered. 'Kiss me.'

If she thought he might hesitate, she was wrong. There was no follow-up question about whether she was sure. He framed her face in his hands and the moment he lowered his lips to hers, that was it. The deal was done and there was no going back. He kissed her until she was dizzy with pleasure and molten with need. Until she began to move in his arms—restlessly seeking the next stage, terrified that any second now he would guess how laughingly inexperienced she was and push her away. She heard him laugh softly as he slid his fingers beneath the sweater to encounter the bra which curved over her breasts.

'Too much clothing,' he murmured, slipping his hand round her back to snap open the offending article and shake it free.

She remembered thinking he must have done this lots of times before and maybe she should confess how innocent she was. But by then he'd started circling her nipples with the light caress of his thumb and the moment passed. Desire pooled like honey in her groin and Keira gave a little cry as sensation threatened to overwhelm her.

'Sta' zitto,' he urged softly as he pulled the sweater over her head and tossed it aside, the movement quickly followed by the efficient disposal of his own T-shirt and boxers. 'Stay quiet. We don't want to disturb the rest of the house, do we?'

Keira shook her head, unable to answer because now he was sliding her panties down and a wild flame of hunger was spreading through her body. 'Matteo,' she gasped as his fingers moved down over her belly and began to explore her molten flesh. He stoked her with a delicacy which was tantalising—each intimate caress making her slide deeper into a brand-new world of intimacy. Yet strangely, it felt familiar. As if she knew exactly what to do, despite being such a novice. Did he tell her to part her legs or were they opening of their own accord? She didn't know. All she knew was that once he started stroking his fingertip against those hot, wet folds, she thought she might pass out with pleasure. 'Oh,' she whispered, on a note of wonder.

'Oh, what?' he murmured.

'It's...incredible.'

'I know it is. Now, touch me,' he urged against her mouth.

Keira swallowed. Did she dare? He was so big and proud and she didn't really know what to do. Swallowing down her nerves, she took him between her thumb and forefinger and began to stroke him up and down with a featherlight motion which nearly made him shoot off the bed.

'*Madonna mia!* Where did you learn to do *that*?' he gasped.

She guessed it might destroy the mood if she explained that car mechanics were often blessed with a naturally sensitive touch. Instead, she enquired in a husky voice which didn't really sound like her voice at all, 'Do you like it?'

'Do I like it?' He swallowed. 'Are you crazy? I love it.'

So why was he halting her progress with the firm clamp of his hand around her wrist, if he loved it so much? Why was he was blindly reaching for the wallet which he'd placed on the nightstand? He was pulling out a small foil packet and Keira shivered as she realised what he was about to do. This might be the craziest and most impulsive thing which had ever happened to her—but at least she would be protected.

He slid on the condom and she was surprised by her lack of fear as she wound her arms eagerly around his neck. Because it felt right. Not because he was rich and powerful, or even because he was insanely good-looking and sexy, but because something about him had touched her heart. Maybe it was the way his voice had softened when he'd asked her those questions about Christmas. Almost as if he *cared*—and it had been a long time since anybody had cared. Was she such a sucker for a few crumbs of affection that she would give herself completely to a man she didn't really know? She wasn't sure. All she knew was that she wanted him more than she'd ever wanted anything.

'Matteo,' she said as he pulled her into his body.

His eyes gleamed as he looked down at her. 'You want to change your mind?'

His consideration only made her want him more. 'No,' she whispered, her fingertips whispering over his neck. 'No way.'

He kissed her again—until she'd reached that same delicious melting point as before and then he moved to straddle her. His face was shadowed as he positioned himself and she tensed as he made that first thrust and began to move, but although the pain was sharp it was thankfully brief. She saw his brow darken and felt him grow very still before he changed his rhythm. His movements slowed as he bent her legs and wrapped them tightly around his waist so that with each long thrust he seemed to fill her completely.

As her body relaxed to accommodate his thickness, Keira felt the excitement build. Inch by glorious inch he entered her, before pulling back to repeat the same sweet stroke, over and over again. She could feel her skin growing heated as all her nerve-endings bunched in exquisitely tight anticipation. She could feel the inexorable build-up of excitement to such a pitch that she honestly didn't think she could take it any more. And then it happened. Like a swollen dam bursting open, waves of intense pleasure began to take her under. She felt herself shatter, as if he needed to break her apart before she could become whole again, and she pressed her mouth against his sweat-sheened shoulder. Dimly, she became aware of his own bucked release as he shuddered above her and was surprised by the unexpected prick of tears to her eyes.

He pulled out of her and rolled back against the pillows to suck in a ragged breath. With a sudden shyness, Keira glanced across at him but his eyes were closed and his olive features shuttered, so that suddenly she felt excluded from the private world in which he seemed to be lost. The room was quiet and she didn't dare speak—wondering what women usually said at moments like this.

Eventually he turned to her, his eyebrows raised in question and an expression on his face she couldn't quite work out.

'So?'

She wanted to hang on to the pleasure for as long as possible—she didn't want it all to evaporate beneath the harsh spotlight of explanation—but he seemed to be waiting for one all the same.

She peered up at him. 'You're angry?'

He shrugged. 'Why should I be angry?'

'Because I didn't tell you.'

'That you were a virgin?' He gave an odd kind of laugh. 'I'm glad you didn't. It might have shattered the mood.'

She tucked a strand of hair behind her ear. 'Aren't you going to ask me why?'

'You chose me to be your first?' His smile now held a faint trace of arrogance. 'I could commend you for your excellent judgment in selecting someone like me to be your first lover, but it's not really any of my business, is it, Keira?'

For some reason, that hurt, though she wasn't going to show it. Had she been naïve enough to suppose he might exhibit a chest-thumping pride that she had chosen him, rather than anyone else? 'I suppose not,' she said, her toes moving beneath the rumpled bed-clothes in a desperate attempt to locate her only pair of panties.

'I just hope you weren't disappointed.'

'You must know I wasn't,' she said, in a small voice.

He seemed to soften a little at that, and brushed back a few little tufts of hair which had fallen untidily over her forehead. '*Sì*, I know. And for what it's worth, it was pretty damned amazing for me, too. I've never had sex with a virgin before but I understand it's uncommon for it to be as good as that the first time. So you should feel very pleased with yourself.' He began to stroke her hair. 'And you're tired.'

'No.'

'Yes,' he said firmly. 'And you need to sleep. So why don't you do that? Lie back and let yourself drift off.'

His words were soothing but Keira didn't want to sleep, she wanted to talk. She wanted to ask him about himself and his life. She wanted to know what would happen now—but there was something in his voice which indicated he didn't feel the same. And mightn't stilted conversation destroy some of this delicious afterglow which felt so impossibly fragile—like a bubble which could be popped at any moment? So she nodded obediently and shut her eyes and within seconds she could feel herself drifting off into the most dreamy sleep she'd ever known.

Matteo watched as her eyelashes fluttered down and waited until her breathing was steady before removing his arm from where it had been resting around her shoulders, but, although she stirred a little, she didn't waken. And that was when the reality of what he'd done hit him.

He'd just seduced a member of staff. More than that, he'd taken her innocence.

Silently, he cursed. He'd broken two fundamental rules in the most spectacular way. His chest was tight as he switched off the lamp and his mind buzzed as he attempted to ignore the naked woman who lay sleeping beside him. Yet that was easier said than done. He wanted nothing more than to push his growing erection inside her tight body again, but he needed to work out the most effective form of damage limitation. For both of them.

He stared up at the shadowy ceiling and sighed. He didn't want to hurt her and he could so easily hurt her. Hurting was something he seemed to do to women without even trying, mainly because he couldn't do love and he couldn't do emotion—at least that was what he'd been accused of, time after time. And Keira didn't deserve that. She'd given herself to him with an openness which had left him breathless and afterwards there had been no demands.

But none of that detracted from the reality of their situation. They came from worlds which were poles apart, which had collided in this small bedroom on the snowy outreaches of Devon. For a brief time they had come together in mindless pleasure but in truth they were nothing more than mismatched strangers driven by the stir of lust. Back in Italy he had been given an ultimatum which needed addressing and he needed to consider the truth behind his father's words.

'Give me an heir, Matteo,' he had breathed. *'Continue the Valenti name and I will give you your heart's desire. Refuse and I will sign the estate over to your stepbrother and his child.'*

Matteo's heart kicked with pain. He had to decide how much he was willing to sacrifice to maintain his links to the past. He needed to return to his world. And Keira to hers.

His jaw tightened. Would he have stopped if he'd known he was her first? He might have *wanted* to stop but something told him he would have been powerless to pull back from the indescribable lure of her petite body. His throat dried as he remembered that first sweet thrust. She had seemed much too small to accommodate him, but she had taken him inside her as if he had been intended to fit into her and only her. He remembered the way she'd touched him with that tentative yet sure touch. She'd made him want to explode. Had the newness of it been responsible for her joyful response—and for the tears which had trickled against his shoulder afterwards, but which she'd hastily blotted away?

Suddenly he could understand the potent power wielded by virgins but he could also recognise that they were a responsibility. They still had dreams—because experience hadn't yet destroyed them. Would she be expecting him to take her number? For him to fly her out to Rome for a weekend of sex and then see what happened? Hand in hand for a sunset stroll along Trastevere, Rome's supposedly most romantic neighbourhood? Because that was never going to happen. His jaw tightened. It would only raise up her hopes before smashing them.

He heard her murmur something in her sleep and felt the heavy weight of his conscience as he batted possibilities back and forth. What would be the best thing he could do for Keira—this sexy little driver with the softest lips he'd ever known? Glancing at his watch, he saw from the luminous dial that it was just before midnight and the rest of the house had grown silent. Could he risk using the landline downstairs without waking everyone? Of course he could. Slipping from the sex-scented bed, he threw on some clothes and made his way downstairs.

He placed the call without any trouble, but his mood was strangely low after he'd terminated his whispered conversation and made his way back to the bedroom. With the light from the corridor flooding in, he stared at Keira's face, which was pillowed on a bent elbow. Her lips were curved in a soft smile and he wanted to kiss them. To take her in his arms and run his hands over her and do it all over again. But he couldn't. Or rather, he shouldn't.

He was careful not to touch her as he climbed into bed, but the thought of her out-of-bounds nakedness meant that he lay there sleeplessly for a long, long time.

CHAPTER FOUR

A PALE LIGHT woke her and for a moment Keira lay completely still, her head resting against a lumpy pillow as her eyes flickered open and she tried to work out exactly where she was. And then she remembered. She was in a strange bedroom on the edge of a snowy Dartmoor—and she'd just lost her virginity to the powerful billionaire she'd been driving around the country!

She registered the sweet aching between her legs and the delicious sting of her nipples as slowly she turned her head to see that the other half of the bed was empty. Her pulse speeded up. He must be in the bathroom. Quickly, she sat up, raking her fingers through her mussed hair and giving herself a chance to compose herself before Matteo returned.

The blindingly pale crack of light shining through the gap in the curtains showed that the snow was still very much in evidence and a smile of anticipation curved her lips. Maybe they'd be stuck here today too—and they could have sex all over again. She certainly hoped so. Crossing her arms over her naked breasts, she hugged herself tightly as endorphins flooded through her warm body. Obviously, she'd need to reassure him that although she was relatively inexperienced, she certainly wasn't naïve. She knew the score—she'd heard the men in the workshop talking about women often enough to know what they did and didn't like. She would be very grown up about what had happened. She'd make it clear that she wasn't coming at this with any *expectations*—although, of course, if he wanted to see her again when the snow had been cleared she would be more than happy with that.

And that was when she noticed the nightstand—or rather, what was lying on top of it. Keira blinked her eyes in disbelief but as her vision cleared she realised this was no illusion as she stared in growing horror at the enormous wad of banknotes. She felt as if she were taking part in some secretly filmed reality show. As if the money might suddenly disintegrate if she touched it, or as if Matteo would suddenly appear from out of hiding. She looked around, realising there *was* nowhere to hide in this tiny room.

'Matteo?' she questioned uncertainly.

Nobody came. Of course they didn't. She stared at the money and then noticed the piece of paper which was lying underneath it. It took several seconds before she could bring herself to pick it up and as she began to read it she was scarcely able to believe what she was seeing.

Keira, he had written—and in the absence of any affectation like *Dear* or *Darling*, she supposed she ought to be grateful that he'd got her name right, because Irish names were notoriously difficult to spell.

I just wanted to tell you how much I enjoyed last night and I hope you did, too. You looked so peaceful sleeping this morning that I didn't want to wake you—but I need to be back in Italy as soon as possible.

You told me your dream was to spend Christmas in a luxury hotel and I'd like to make this possible, which is why I hope you'll accept this small gift in the spirit with which it was intended.

And if we'd been playing poker for money, you would certainly have walked away with a lot more than this!

I wish you every good thing for your future. Buon Natale. Matteo.

Keira's fingers closed tightly around the note and her feeling of confusion intensified as she stared at the money—more money than she'd ever seen. She allowed herself a moment of fury before getting up out of bed, acutely aware that for once she wasn't wearing her usual nightshirt, and the sight of her naked body in the small mirror taunted her with memories of just what she and the Italian had done last night. And once the fury had passed she was left with hurt, and disappointment. Had she really been lying there, naïvely thinking that Matteo was going to emerge from the bathroom and take her in his arms when the reality was that he couldn't even bear to face her? What a stupid fool she'd been.

She washed and dressed and went downstairs, politely refusing breakfast but accepting a mug of strong tea from Mary, who seemed delighted to relay every-thing which had been happening while Keira had been asleep.

'First thing I know, there's a knock on the door and it's a man in one of those big four-wheel drives,' she announced.

'Which managed to get through the snow?' questioned Keira automatically.

'Oh, yes. Because Mr Valenti ordered a car with a snow plough. Apparently he got on the phone late last night while everyone was asleep and organised it. Must have been very quiet because nobody heard him.'

Very quiet, thought Keira grimly. He must have been terrified that she would wake up and demand he take her with him.

'And he's ordered some men to dig your car out of the snow. Said there was no way you must be stranded here,' said Mary, with a dreamy look on her careworn face. 'They arrived about an hour ago—they should be finished soon.'

Keira nodded. 'Can I pay you?'

Mary beamed. 'No need. Your Mr Valenti was more than generous.'

Keira's heart pounded; she wanted to scream that he wasn't 'her' anything. So the cash wasn't there to pay for the B& B or help her make her own journey home, because he'd already sorted all that out. Which left only one reason for leaving it. Of course. How could she have been so dense when the bland words of the accompanying letter had made it perfectly clear? The comment about the poker and the disingenuous suggestion she take herself off to a luxury hotel were just a polite way of disguising the very obvious. A wave of sickness washed over her.

Matteo Valenti had *paid her for sex*.

Operating on a dazed kind of autopilot, Keira made her way back to her newly liberated car, from where she slowly drove back to London. After dropping the car off at Luxury Limos, she made her way to Brixton, acutely aware of the huge wad of cash she was carrying. She'd thought of leaving it behind at Mary's, but wouldn't the kindly landlady have tried to return it and just made matters a whole lot worse? And how on earth would she have managed to explain what it was doing there? Yet it felt as if it were burning a massive hole in her pocket—haunting her with the bitter reminder of just what the Italian really thought of her.

The area of Brixton where she rented a tiny apartment had once been considered unfashionable but now, like much of London, the place was on the up. Two days before Christmas and the streets had a festive air which was bordering on the hysterical, despite the fact that the heavy snows hadn't reached the capital. Bright lights glittered and she could see Christmas trees and scarlet-suited Santas everywhere she looked. On the corner, a Salvation Army band was playing 'Silent Night' and the poignancy of the familiar tune made her heart want to break. And stupidly, she found herself missing her mother like never before as she thought about all the Christmases they'd never got to share. Tears pricked at the backs of her eyes as she hugged her anorak around her shivering body, and never had she felt so completely alone.

But self-pity would get her nowhere. She was a survivor, wasn't she? She would get through this as she had got through so much else. Dodging the crowds, she started to walk home, her journey taking her past one of the area's many charity shops and as an idea came to her she impulsively pushed open the door of one. Inside, the place was full of people trying on clothes for Christmas parties and New Year—raiding feather boas and old-fashioned shimmery dresses from the crowded rails. The atmosphere was chaotic and happy but Keira was grim-faced as she made her way to the cash desk. Fumbling around in her pocket, she withdrew the wad of cash and slapped it down on the counter in front of the startled cashier.

'Take this,' Keira croaked. 'And Happy Christmas.'

The woman held up a hand. 'Whoa! Wait a minute! Where did you—?'

But Keira was already pushing her way out of the shop, the cold air hitting the tears which had begun streaming down her cheeks. Her vision blurred and she stumbled a little and might have fallen if a steady arm hadn't caught her elbow.

'Are you okay?' a female voice was saying.

Was she okay? No, she most definitely was not. Keira nodded, looking up at a woman with platinum hair who was wearing a leopard-skin-print coat. 'I'm fine. I just need to get home,' she husked.

'Not like that, you're not. You're not fit to go anywhere,' said the woman firmly. 'Let me buy you a drink. You look like you could use one.'

Still shaken, Keira allowed herself to be led into the bright interior of the Dog and Duck where music was playing and the smell of mulled wine filled her nostrils. The woman went up to the bar and returned minutes later with a glass of a brown mixture resembling medicine, which was pushed across the scratched surface of the table towards her.

'What's this?' Keira mumbled, lifting the glass and recoiling from the fumes.

'Brandy.'

'I don't like brandy.'

'Drink it. You look like you're in shock.'

That much was true. Keira took a large and fiery swallow and the weird thing was that she *did* feel better afterwards. Disorientated, yes—but better.

'So where did you get the money from?' the blonde was asking. 'Did you rob a bank or something? I was in the charity shop when you came in and handed it over. Pretty dramatic gesture, but a lovely thing to do, I must say—especially at this time of the year.'

Afterwards Keira thought that if she hadn't had the brandy then she might not have told the sympathetic blonde the whole story, but the words just started tumbling out of her mouth and they wouldn't seem to stop. Just like the tears which had preceded them. It was only when the woman's eyes widened when she came out with the punchline about how Matteo had left her a stack of money and done a runner that she became aware that something in the atmosphere had changed.

'So he just disappeared? Without a word?'

'Well, he left a note.'

'May I see it?'

Keira put the brandy glass down with a thud. 'No.'

There was a pause. 'He must be very rich,' observed the blonde. 'To be able to be carrying around that kind of money.'

Keira shrugged. 'Very.'

'And good-looking, I suppose?'

Keira swallowed. 'What does that have to do with anything?'

The blonde's heavily made-up eyes narrowed. 'Hunky Italian billionaires don't usually have to pay women for sex.'

It was hearing someone else say it out loud which made it feel a million times worse—something Keira hadn't actually thought possible. She rose unsteadily to her feet, terrified she was going to start gagging. 'I... I'm going home now,' she whispered. 'Please forget I said anything. And...thanks for the drink.'

Somehow she managed to get home unscathed, where her cold, bare bedsit showed no signs of the impending holiday. She'd been so busy that she hadn't even bought herself a little tree, but that now seemed like the least of her worries. She realised she hadn't checked her phone messages since she'd got back and found a terse communication from her aunt, asking her what time she was planning on turning up on Christmas Day and hoping she hadn't forgotten to buy the pudding.

The pudding! Now she would have to brave the wretched shops again. Keira closed her eyes as she pictured the grim holiday which lay ahead of her. How was she going to get through a whole Christmas, nursing the shameful secret of what she'd done?

Her phone began to ring, the small screen flashing an unknown number; in an effort to distract herself with the inevitable sales call, Keira accepted the call with a tentative hello. There was an infinitesimal pause before a male voice spoke.

'Keira?'

It was a voice she hadn't known until very recently but she thought that rich, Italian accent would be branded on her memory until the end of time. Dark and velvety, it whispered over her skin just as his fingers had done. Matteo! And despite everything—the wad of money and the blandly worded note and the fact that he'd left without even saying goodbye—wasn't there a great lurch of hope inside her foolish heart? She pictured his ruffled hair and the dark eyes which had gleamed with passion when they'd looked at her. The way he'd crushed his lips hungrily down on hers, and that helpless moment of bliss when he'd first entered her.

'Matteo?'

Another pause—and if a silence could ever be considered ominous, this one was. 'So how much did she pay you?' he questioned.

'Pay me?' Keira blinked in confusion, thinking that bringing up money wasn't the best way to start a conversation, especially in view of what had happened. 'What are you talking about?'

'I've just had a phone call from a…a *journalist*.'

He spat out the word as if it were poison. 'Asking me whether I make a habit of paying women for sex.'

Keira's feeling of confusion intensified. 'I don't...' And then she realised and hot colour flooded into her cheeks. 'Was her name Hester?'

'So you *did* speak to her?' He sucked in an unsteady breath. 'What was it, Keira—a quickly arranged interview to see what else you could squeeze out of me?'

'I didn't plan on talking to her—it just happened.'

'Oh, really?'

'Yes, really. I was angry about the money you left me!' she retorted.

'Why? Didn't you think it was enough?' he shot back. 'Did you imagine you might be able to get even more?'

Keira sank onto the nearest chair, terrified that her wobbly legs were going to give way beneath her. 'You bastard,' she whispered.

'Your anger means nothing to me,' he said coldly. 'For *you* are nothing to me. I wasn't thinking straight. I couldn't have been thinking straight. I should never have had sex with you because I don't make a habit of having one-night stands with strangers. But what's done can't be undone and I have only myself to blame.'

There was a pause before he resumed and now his voice had taken on a flat and implacable note, which somehow managed to sound even more ominous than his anger.

'I've told your journalist friend that if she prints one word about me, I'll go after her and bring her damned publication down,' he continued. 'Because I'm not someone you can blackmail—I'm just a man who allowed himself to be swayed by lust and it's taught me a lesson I'm never going to forget.' He gave a bitter laugh. 'So, goodbye, Keira. Have a good life.'

CHAPTER FIVE

Ten months later

'I HOPE THAT baby isn't going to cry all the way through lunch, Keira. It would be nice if we were able to eat a meal in peace for once.'

Tucking little Santino into the crook of her arm, Keira nodded as she met her aunt's accusing stare. She would have taken the baby out for a walk if the late October day hadn't been so foul and blustery. Or she might have treated him to a long bus ride to lull him to sleep if he hadn't been so tiny. As it was, she was stuck in the house with a woman who seemed determined to find fault in everything she did, and she was tired. So tired. With the kind of tiredness which seemed to have seeped deep into her bones and taken up residence there. 'I'll try to put him down for his nap before we sit down to eat,' she said hopefully.

Aunt Ida's mouth turned down at the corners, emphasising the deep grooves of discontentment which hardened her thin face. 'That'll be a first. Poor Shelley says she hasn't had an unbroken night since you moved in. He's obviously an unsettled baby if he cries so much. Maybe it's time you came to your senses and thought about adoption.'

Keira's teeth dug into her bottom lip as the word lodged like a barb in her skin.

Adoption.

A wave of nausea engulfed her but she tried very hard not to react as she stared down into the face of her sleeping son. Holding onto Santino even tighter, she felt her heart give a savage lurch of love as she told herself to ignore the snide comments and concentrate on what was important. Because only one thing mattered and that was her baby son.

Everything you do is for him, she reminded herself fiercely. *Everything.* No point in wishing she hadn't given away Matteo's money, or tormenting herself by thinking how useful it might have been. She hadn't known at the time that she was pregnant—how could she have done? She'd handed over that thick wad of banknotes as if there were loads more coming her way—and now she just had to deal with the situation as it was and not what it could have been. She had to accept that she'd lost her job and her home in quick succession and had been forced to take the charity of a woman who had always disapproved of her. Because how else would she and Santino have managed to cope in an uncaring and hostile world?

You know exactly how, prompted the ever-present voice of her conscience but Keira pushed it from her mind. She could *not* have asked Matteo for help, not when he had treated her like some kind of *whore*. Who had made it clear he never wanted to see her again.

'Have you registered the child's birth yet?' Aunt Ida was asking.

'Not yet, no,' said Keira. 'I have to do it within the first six weeks.'

'Better get a move on, then.'

Keira waited, knowing that there was more.

Her aunt smiled slyly. 'Only I was wondering whether you were going to put the mystery father's name on the birth certificate—or whether you were like your poor dear mother and didn't actually know who he was?'

Keira's determination not to react drained away. Terrified of saying something she might later regret, she turned and walked out of the sitting room without another word, glad she was holding Santino because that stopped her from picking up one of her aunt's horrible china ornaments and hurling it against the wall. Criticism directed against her she could just about tolerate—but she wouldn't stand to hear her mother's name maligned like that.

Her anger had evaporated by the time she reached the box-room she shared with Santino, and Keira placed the baby carefully in his crib, tucking the edges of the blanket around his tiny frame and staring at him. His lashes looked very long and dark against his olive skin but for once she found herself unable to take pleasure in his innocent face. Because suddenly, the fear and the guilt which had been nagging away inside her now erupted into one fierce and painful certainty.

She couldn't go on like this. Santino deserved more than a mother who was permanently exhausted, having to tiptoe around a too-small house with people who didn't really like her. She closed her eyes, knowing there was somebody else who didn't like her—but someone she suspected wouldn't display a tight-lipped intolerance whenever the baby started to cry. Because it was *his* baby, too. And didn't all parents love their children, no matter what?

A powerful image swam into her mind of a man whose face she could picture without too much trying. She knew what she had to do. Something she'd thought about doing every day since Santino's birth, and in the nine months preceding it, until she'd forced herself to remember how unequivocally he'd told her he never wanted to see her again. Well, maybe he was going to have to.

Her fingers were shaking as she scrolled down her phone's contact list and retrieved the number she had saved, even though the caller had hung up on her the last time she'd spoken to him.

With a thundering heart, she punched out the number. And waited.

Rain lashed against the car windscreen and flurries of falling leaves swirled like the thoughts in Matteo's mind as his chauffeur-driven limousine drove down the narrow suburban road. As they passed houses which all looked exactly the same, he tried to get his head round what he'd learned during a phone call from a woman he'd never thought he'd see again.

He was a father.

He had a child.

A son. His heart pumped. In a single stroke he had been given exactly what he needed—though not necessarily what he wanted—and could now produce the grandson his father yearned for.

Matteo ordered the driver to stop, trying to dampen down the unfamiliar emotions which were sweeping through his body. And trying to curb his rising temper about the way Keira had kept this news secret. How *dared* she keep his baby hidden and play God with his future? Grim-faced, he stepped out onto the rain-soaked pavement and a wave of determination washed over him as he slammed the car door shut. He was here now and he would fix this—to his advantage. Whatever it took, he would get what he wanted—and he wanted his son.

He hadn't told Keira he was coming. He hadn't wanted to give her the opportunity to elude him. He wanted to surprise her—as she had surprised him. To allow her no time to mount any defences. If she was unprepared and vulnerable then surely that would aid him in his determination to get his rightful heir. Moving stealthily up the narrow path, he rapped a small bronze knocker fashioned in the shape of a lion's head and moments later the door was opened by a woman with tight, curly hair and a hard, lined face.

'Yes?' she said sharply. 'We don't buy from the doorstep.'

'Good afternoon,' he said. Forcing the pleasantry to his unwilling lips, he accompanied it with a polite smile. 'I'm not selling anything. I'd like to see Keira.'

'And you are?'

'My name is Matteo Valenti,' he said evenly. 'And I am her baby's father.'

The woman gasped, her eyes scanning him from head to toe, as if registering his cashmere coat and handmade shoes. Her eyes skated over his shoulder and she must have observed the shiny black car parked so incongruously among all the sedate family saloons. Was he imagining the look of calculation which had hardened her gimlet eyes? Probably not, he thought grimly.

'You?' she demanded.

'That's right,' he agreed, still in that same even voice which betrayed nothing of his growing irritation.

'I had no idea that...' She swallowed. 'I'll have to check if she'll see you.'

'No,' Matteo interrupted her, only just resisting the desire to step forward and jam his foot in the door, like a bailiff. 'I *will* see Keira—and my baby—and it's probably best if we do it with the minimum of fuss.' He glanced behind him where he could see the twitching of net curtains on the opposite side of the road and when he returned his gaze to the woman, his smile was bland. 'Don't you agree? For everyone's sake?'

The woman hesitated before nodding, as if she too had no desire for a scene on the doorstep. 'Very well. You'd better come in.' She cleared her throat. 'I'll let Keira know you're here.'

He was shown into a small room crammed with porcelain figurines but Matteo barely paid any attention to his surroundings. His eyes were trained on the door as it clicked open and he held his breath in anticipation—

expelling it in a long sigh of disbelief and frustration when Keira finally walked in. Frustration because she was alone. And disbelief because he scarcely recognised her as the same woman whose bed he had shared almost a year ago—though that lack of recognition certainly didn't seem to be affecting the powerful jerk of his groin.

Gone was the short, spiky hair and in its place was a dark curtain of silk which hung glossily down to her shoulders. And her body. He swallowed. What the hell had happened to *that*? All the angular leanness of before had gone. Suddenly she had hips—as well as the hint of a belly and breasts. It made her look softer, he thought, until he reminded himself that a woman with any degree of softness wouldn't have done what she had done.

'Matteo,' she said, her voice sounding strained—and it was then he noticed the pallor and the faint circles which darkened the skin beneath her eyes. In those fathomless pools of deepest blue he could read the vulnerability he had wanted to see, yet he felt a sudden twist of something like compassion, until he remembered what she had done.

'The very same,' he agreed grimly. 'Pleased to see me?'

'I wasn't—' She was trying to smile but failing spectacularly. 'I wasn't expecting you. I mean, not like this. Not without any warning.'

'Really? What did you imagine was going to happen, Keira? That I would just accept the news you finally saw fit to tell me and wait for your next instruction?' He walked across the room to stare out of the window and saw that a group of small boys had gathered around his limousine. He turned around and met her eyes. 'Perhaps you were hoping you wouldn't have to see me at all. Were you hoping I would remain a shadowy figure in the background and become your convenient benefactor?'

'Of course I wasn't!'

'No?' He flared his nostrils. 'Then why *bother* telling me about my son? Why now after all these months of secrecy?'

Keira tried not to flinch beneath the accusing gaze which washed over her like a harsh ebony spotlight. It was difficult enough seeing him again and registering the infuriating fact that her body had automatically started to melt, without having to face his undiluted fury.

Remember the things he said to you, she reminded herself. But the memory of his wounding words seemed to have faded and all she could think was the fact that here stood Santino's father and that, oh, the apple didn't fall far from the tree.

For here was the adult version of the little baby she'd just rocked off to sleep before the doorbell had rung. Santino was the image of his father, with his golden olive skin and dark hair, and hadn't the midwife already commented on the fact that her son was going to grow up to be a heartbreaker? Keira swallowed. Just like Matteo.

She felt an uncomfortable rush of awareness because it wasn't easy to acknowledge the stir of her body, or the fact that her senses suddenly felt as if they'd been kicked into life. Matteo's hair and his eyes seemed even blacker than she remembered and never had his sensual lips appeared more kissable. Yet surely that was the last thing she should be thinking of right now. Her mind-set should be fixed on practicalities, not foolish yearnings. She felt disappointed in herself and wondered if nature was clever enough to make a woman desire the father of her child, no matter how contemptuously he was looking at her.

She found herself wishing he'd given her some kind of warning so she could at least have washed her hair and made a bit of effort with her appearance. Since having a baby she'd developed curves and she was shamefully aware that her pre-pregnancy jeans were straining at the hips and her baggy top was deeply unflattering. But the way she looked had been the last thing on her mind. She knew she needed new clothes but she'd been forced to wait, and not just because of a chronic shortage of funds.

Because how could she possibly go shopping for clothes with a tiny infant in tow? Asking her aunt to babysit hadn't been an option—not when she was constantly made aware of their generosity in providing a home for her and her illegitimate child, and how that same child had disrupted all their lives. The truth was she hadn't wanted to spend her precious pennies on new clothes when she could be buying stuff for Santino. Which was why she was wearing an unflattering outfit, which was probably making Matteo Valenti wonder what he'd ever seen in her. Measured against his made-to-measure sophistication, Keira felt like a scruffy wrongdoer who had just been dragged before an elegant high court judge.

She forced a polite smile to her lips. 'Would you like to sit down?'

'No, I don't want to *sit down*. I want an answer to my question. Why did you contact me to tell me that I was a father? Why now?'

She flushed right up to the roots of her hair. 'Because by law I have to register his birth and that brought everything to a head. I've realised I can't go on living like this. I thought I could but I was wrong. I'm very…grateful to my aunt for taking me in but it's too cramped. They don't really want me here and I can kind of see their point.' She met his eyes. 'And I don't want Santino growing up in this kind of atmosphere.'

Santino.

As she said the child's name Matteo felt a whisper of something he didn't recognise. Something completely outside his experience. He could feel it in the icing of his skin and sudden clench of his heart. 'Santino?' he repeated, wondering if he'd misheard her. He stared at her, his brow creased in a frown. 'You gave him an Italian name?'

'Yes.'

'Why?'

'Because when I looked at him—' her voice faltered as she scraped her fingers back through her hair and turned those big sapphire eyes on him '—I knew I could call him nothing else but an Italian name.'

'Even though you sought to deny him his heritage and kept his birth hidden from me?'

She swallowed. 'You made it very clear that you never wanted to see me again, Matteo.'

'I didn't know you were pregnant at the time,' he bit out.

'And neither did I!' she shot back.

'But you knew afterwards.'

'Yes.' How could she explain the sense of alienation she'd felt—not just from him, but from everyone? When everything had seemed so *unreal* and the world had suddenly looked like a very different place. The head of Luxury Limos had said he didn't think it was a good idea if she carried on driving—not when she looked as if she was about to throw up whenever the car went over a bump. And even though she hadn't been sick— not once—and even though Keira knew that by law she could demand to stay where she was, she didn't have the energy or the funds to investigate further. What was she going to do—take him to an industrial tribunal?

She'd been terrified her boss would find out who the father of her unborn child was—because having sex with your most prestigious client was definitely a sacking offence. He'd offered her a job back in the workshop, but she had no desire to slide underneath a car and get oil all over her hands, not when such a precious bundle was growing inside her. Eventually she'd accepted a mind-numbingly dull job behind the reception desk, becoming increasingly aware that on the kind of wages she was being paid, she'd never be able to afford childcare after the birth. She'd saved every penny she could and been as frugal as she knew how, but gradually all her funds were running out and now she was in real trouble.

'Yes, I knew,' she said slowly. 'Just like I knew I ought to tell you that you were going to be a father. But every time I picked up the phone to call you, something held me back. Can't you understand?'

'Frankly, no. I can't.'

She looked him straight in the eye. 'You think those cruel words you said to me last time we spoke wouldn't matter? That you could say what you liked and it wouldn't hurt, or have consequences?'

His voice grew hard. 'I haven't come here to argue the rights and wrongs of your secrecy. I've come to see my son.'

'He's sleeping.'

'I won't wake him.' His voice grew harsh. 'You've denied me all this time and you will deny me no longer. I want to see my son, Keira, and if I have to search every room in the house to find him, then that's exactly what I'm going to do.'

It was a demand Keira couldn't ignore and not just because she didn't doubt his threat to search the small house from top to bottom. She'd seen the brief tightening of his face when she'd mentioned his child and another wave of guilt had washed over her. Because she of all people knew what it was like to grow up without a father. She knew about the gaping hole it left—a hole which could never be filled. And yet she had sought to subject her own child to that.

'Come with me,' she said huskily.

He followed her up the narrow staircase and Keira

was acutely aware of his presence behind her. You couldn't ignore him, even when you couldn't see him, she thought despairingly. She could detect the heat from his body and the subtle sandalwood which was all his and, stupidly, she remembered the way that scent had clung to her skin the morning after he'd made love to her. Her heart was thundering by the time they reached the box-room she shared with Santino and she held her breath as Matteo stood frozen for a moment before moving soundlessly towards the crib. His shoulders were stiff with tension as he reached it and he was silent for so long that she started to get nervous.

'Matteo?' she said.

Matteo didn't answer. Not then. He wasn't sure he trusted himself to speak because his thoughts were in such disarray. He looked down at the baby expecting to feel the instant bolt of love people talked about when they first set eyes on their own flesh and blood, but there was nothing. He stared down at the dark fringe of eyelashes which curved on the infant's olive-hued cheeks and the shock of black hair. Tiny hands were curled into two tiny fists and he found himself leaning forward to count all the fingers, nodding his head with satisfaction as he registered each one. He felt as if he were observing himself and his reaction from a distance and realised it was possession he felt, not love. The sense that this was someone who belonged to him in a way that nobody ever had before.

His son.

He swallowed.

His *son.*

He waited for a moment before turning to Keira and he saw her dark blue eyes widen, as if she'd read something in his face she would prefer not to have seen.

'So you played God with all our futures,' he observed softly. 'By keeping him from me.'

Her gaze became laced with defiance.

'You paid me for sex.'

'I did not *pay you for sex*,' he gritted out. 'I explained my motivation in my note. You spoke of a luxury you weren't used to and I thought I would make it possible. Was that so very wrong?'

'You know very well it was!' she burst out. 'Because offering me cash was insulting. Any man would know that.'

'Was that why you tried to sell your story to the journalist, because you felt "insulted"?'

'I did not *sell my story* to anyone,' she shot back. 'Can't you imagine what it was like? I'd had sex for the first time and woke to find you gone, leaving that wretched pile of money. I walked into a charity shop to get rid of it because it felt…well, it felt tainted, if you must know.'

He grew very still. 'You gave it away?'

'Yes, I gave it away. To a worthy cause—to children living in care. Not realising I was pregnant at the time and could have used the money myself. The journalist just happened to be in the shop and overheard—and naturally she was interested. She bought me a drink and I hadn't eaten anything all day and…' She shrugged. 'I guess I told her more than I meant to.'

Matteo's eyes narrowed. If her story was true it

meant she hadn't tried to grab some seedy publicity from their brief liaison. *If it was true.* Yet even if it was—did it really change anything? He was here only because her back was up against the wall and she had nowhere else to turn. His gaze swept over the too-tight jeans and baggy jumper. And this was the mother of his child, he thought, his lips curving with distaste.

He opened his mouth to speak but Santino chose that moment to start to whimper and Keira bent over the crib to scoop him up, whispering her lips against his hair and rocking him in her arms until he had grown quiet again. She looked over his head, straight into Matteo's eyes. 'Would you...would you like to hold him?'

Matteo went very still. He knew he *should* want that, but although he thought it, he still couldn't *feel* it. There was nothing but an icy lump where his heart should have been and as he looked at his son he couldn't shift that strange air of detachment.

His lack of emotional empathy had never mattered to him before—only his frustrated lovers had complained about it and that had never been reason enough to change, or even *want* to change. But now he felt like someone on a beach who had inadvertently stepped onto quicksand. As if matters were spinning beyond his control.

And he needed to assert control, just as he always did.

Of course he would hold his son when he'd got his head round the fact that he actually *had* a son. But it would be in conditions favourable to them both—not in some tiny bedroom of a strange house while Keira stood studying him with those big blue eyes.

'Not now,' he said abruptly. 'There isn't time. You need to pack your things while I call ahead and prepare for your arrival in Italy.'

'*What?*'

'You heard me. He isn't staying here. And since a child needs a mother, then I guess you will have to come, too.'

'What are you talking about?' She rocked the child against her breast. 'I know it's not perfect here but I can't just walk out without making any plans. We can't just go to *Italy.*'

'You can't put out a call for help and then ignore help when it comes. You telephoned me and now you must accept the consequences,' he added grimly. 'You've already implied that the atmosphere here is intolerable so I'm offering you an alternative. The only sensible alternative.' He pulled a mobile phone from the pocket of his cashmere overcoat and began to scroll down the numbers. 'For a start, you need a nursery nurse to help you.'

'I don't *need* a nurse,' she contradicted fiercely. 'Women like me don't have nurses. They look after their babies themselves.'

'Have you looked in the mirror recently?'

It was an underhand blow to someone who was already feeling acutely sensitive and once again Keira flushed. 'I'm sorry I didn't have a chance to slap on a whole load of make-up and put on a party dress!'

He shook his head. 'That wasn't what I meant. You look as if you haven't had a decent night's sleep in weeks and I'm giving you the chance to get some rest.' He forced himself to be gentle with her, even though his instinct was always to push for exactly what he wanted. And yet strangely, he felt another wave of compassion as he looked into her pale face. 'Now, we can do this one of two ways. You can fight me or you can make the best of the situation and come willingly.' His mouth flattened. 'But if you choose the former, it will be fruitless because I want this, Keira. I want it very badly. And when I want something, I usually get it. Do you believe me?'

The mulish look which entered her eyes was there for only a second before she gave a reluctant nod. 'Yes,' she said grudgingly. 'I believe you.'

'Then pack what you need and I'll wait downstairs.' He turned away but was halted by the sound of her voice.

'And when we get there, what happens then, Matteo?' she whispered. 'To Santino?' There was a pause. 'To us?'

He didn't turn back. He didn't want to look at her right then, or tell her he didn't think there was an 'us'. 'I have no crystal ball,' he ground out. 'We'll just have to make it up as we go along. Now pack your things.'

He went downstairs, and, despite telling himself that this was nothing more than a problem which needed solving, he could do nothing about the sudden and inexplicable wrench of pain in his heart. But years of practice meant he had composed himself long before he reached the tiny hallway and his face was as hard as granite as he let himself out into the rainy English day.

CHAPTER SIX

GOLDEN SUNLIGHT DANCED on her closed eyelids and warmed her skin as Keira nestled back into the comfortable lounger. The only sounds she could hear were birdsong and the buzz of bees and, in the far distance, the crowing of a cock—even though it was the middle of the day. Hard to believe she'd left behind a rain-washed English autumn to arrive in a country where it was still warm enough to sit outside in October. And even harder to believe that she was at Matteo Valenti's Umbrian estate, with its acres of olive groves, award-winning vineyards and breathtaking views over mountains and lake. In his private jet, he'd announced he was bringing her here, to his holiday home, to 'acclimatise' herself before he introduced her to his real life in Rome. She hadn't been sure what he meant by that but she'd been too exhausted to raise any objections. She'd been here a week and much of that time had been spent asleep, or making sure that Santino was content. It felt like being transplanted to a luxury spa cleverly hidden within a rustic setting—with countless people working quietly in the background to maintain the estate's smooth running.

At first she'd been too preoccupied with the practical elements of settling in with her baby to worry about the emotional repercussions of being there. She'd worried about the little things, like how Matteo would react when he discovered she wasn't feeding Santino herself. Whether he would judge her negatively, as the whole world seemed to do if a woman couldn't manage to breastfeed. Was that why, in a rare moment of candour, she'd found herself explaining how ill she'd been after the birth—which meant breastfeeding hadn't been possible? She thought she'd glimpsed a brief softening of the granite-like features before his rugged features resumed their usual implacable mask.

'It will be easier that way,' he'd said, with a shrug. 'Easier for the nursery nurse.'

How *cold* he could be, she thought. Even if he was right. Because despite her earlier resistance, she was now hugely appreciative of the nursery nurse they'd employed. The very day after they'd arrived, he had produced three candidates for her to interview—topnotch women who had graduated from Italy's finest training establishment and who all spoke fluent English. After asking them about a million questions—but more importantly watching to see how well they interacted with her baby—Keira had chosen Claudia, a serene woman in her mid-thirties whom she instinctively trusted. It meant Keira got all the best bits of being a mother—cuddling and bathing her adorable son and making goo-goo noises at him as she walked him around the huge estate—while Claudia took over the dreaded three o'clock morning feed.

Which meant she could catch up with the sleep she so badly needed. She'd felt like a complete zombie when she arrived—a fact not helped by the disorientating experience of being flown to Italy on Matteo's luxury jet then being picked up by the kind of limousine which only a year ago she would have been chauffeuring. The drive to his Umbrian property had passed in a blur and Keira remembered thinking that the only time emotion had entered Matteo's voice was when they drove through the ancient gates and he began to point out centuries-old landmarks, with an unmistakable sense of pride and affection.

She almost wished Santino had been a little older so he could have appreciated the silvery ripple of olive trees, heavy with fruit and ready for harvest, and the golden pomegranates which hung from the branches like Christmas baubles. She remembered being greeted by a homely housekeeper named Paola and the delicious hot bath she took once the baby had been settled. There had been the blissful sensation of sliding between crisp, clean sheets and laying her head on a pillow of goosedown, followed by her first full night's sleep since before the birth. And that was pretty much how she'd spent the last seven days, feeling her vitality and strength returning with each hour that passed.

'You're smiling,' came a richly accented voice from above her as a shadow suddenly blotted out the sun.

Shielding her eyes with the edge of her hand, Keira peered up to see Matteo towering over her and her smile instantly felt as if it had become frozen. She could feel her heart picking up speed and the tug of silken hunger in the base of her belly and silently she cursed the instinctive reaction of her body. Because as her strength had returned, so too had her desire for Matteo—a man who she couldn't quite decide was her jailer or her saviour. Or both.

Their paths hadn't crossed much because he'd spent much of the time working in a distant part of the enormous farmhouse. It was as if he'd unconsciously marked out different territories for them, with clear demarcation lines which couldn't be crossed. But what she'd noted above all else was the fact that he'd kept away from the nursery, using the *excuse* that his son needed to settle in before getting used to too many new people. Because that was what it had sounded like. An excuse. A reason not to touch the son he had insisted should come here.

She'd seen him, of course. Glimpses in passing, which had unsettled her. Matteo looking brooding and muscular in faded denims and a shirt as he strode about the enormous estate, conversing in rapid Italian with his workers—or wearing a knockout charcoal suit just before driving to Rome for the day and returning long after she'd gone to bed.

Another image was burnt vividly into her mind, too. She'd overslept one morning and gone straight to the nursery to find Claudia cradling Santino by the window and telling him to watch 'Papa' going down the drive. *Papa.* It was a significant word. It emphasised Matteo's importance in their lives yet brought home how little she really knew about the cold-hearted billionaire. Yet that hadn't stopped her heart from missing a beat as he'd speeded out of the estate in his gleaming scarlet sports car, had it?

'It makes me realise how rarely I see you smile,' observed Matteo, still looking down at her as he stood silhouetted by the rich October sun.

'Maybe that's because we've hardly seen one another,' said Keira, flipping on the sunglasses which had been perched on top of her head, grateful for the way they kept her expression hidden. Not for the first time, she found it almost impossible to look at the man in front of her with any degree of impartiality, but she disguised it with a cool look. 'And you're a fine one to talk about smiling. You don't exactly go around the place grinning from ear to ear, do you?'

'Perhaps our forthcoming trip to Rome might bring a smile to both our faces,' he suggested silkily.

Ah yes, the trip to Rome. Keira felt the anxious slam of her heart. She licked her lips. 'I've been meaning to talk to you about that. Do we really have to go?'

In a movement which distractingly emphasised the jut of his narrow hips, he leaned against the sun-baked wall of the farmhouse. 'We've agreed to this, Keira. You need to see the other side of my life, not just this rural idyll. And I'm mainly based in Rome.'

'And the difference is what?'

'It's a high-octane city and nothing like as relaxed as here. When I'm there I go to restaurants and theatres. I have friends there and get invited to parties—and as the mother of my baby, I will be taking you with me.'

She sat up on the lounger, anxiety making her heart thud even harder against her ribcage. 'Why bother?

Why not just leave me somewhere in the background and concentrate on forming a relationship with your son?'

'I think we have to examine all the possibilities,' he said carefully. 'And number one on that list is to work out whether we could have some kind of life together.' He lifted his brows. 'It would certainly make things a whole lot easier.'

'And you're saying I'll let you down in my current state, is that it?'

He shrugged his broad shoulders with a carelessness which wasn't very convincing. 'I think we're both aware that you don't have a suitable wardrobe for that kind of lifestyle. You can't wear jeans all the time and Paola mentioned that you only seem to have one pair of boots.'

'So Paola's been spying on me, has she?' Keira questioned, her voice dipping with disappointment that the genial housekeeper seemed to have been taking her inventory.

'Don't be absurd. She was going to clean them for you and couldn't find any others you could wear in the meantime.'

Keira scrambled up off the lounger and stared into his hard and beautiful features. He really came from a totally different planet, didn't he? One which was doubtless inhabited by women who had boots in every colour of the rainbow and not just a rather scuffed brown pair she'd bought in the sales. 'So don't take me with you,' she said flippantly. 'Leave me behind while you go out to all your fancy places and I can stay home and look after Santino, wearing my solitary pair of boots.'

A flicker of a smile touched the corners of his lips, but just as quickly it was gone. 'That isn't an option, I'm afraid,' he said smoothly. 'You're going to have to meet people. Not just my friends and the people who work for me, but my father and stepmother at some point. And my stepbrother,' he finished, his mouth twisting before his gaze fixed her with its ebony blaze. 'The way you look at the moment means you won't fit in. Not anywhere,' he continued brutally. 'And there's the chance that people will talk about you if you behave like some kind of hermit, which won't make things easy for you. Apart from anything else, we need to learn more about each other.' He hesitated. 'We are parents, with a child and a future to consider. We need to discuss the options open to us and that won't be possible if we continue to be strangers to one another.'

'You haven't bothered coming near me since we got here,' she said quietly. 'You've been keeping your distance, haven't you?'

'Can you blame me? You were almost on your knees with exhaustion when you arrived.' He paused as his eyes swept over her again. 'But you look like a different person now.'

Keira was taken aback by the way her body responded to that slow scrutiny, wondering how he could make her feel so many different things, simply by looking at her. And if that was the case, shouldn't she be protecting herself from his persuasive power over her, instead of going on a falsely intimate trip to Rome?

'I told you. I don't want to leave the baby,' she said stubbornly.

'Is that what's known as playing your trump card?' he questioned softly. 'Making me out to be some cruel tyrant who's dragging you away from your child?'

'He's only little! Not that you'd know, of course.' She paused and lifted her chin. 'You've hardly gone near him.'

Matteo acknowledged the unmistakable challenge in her voice and he felt a sudden chill ice his skin, despite the warmth of the October day. How audacious of her to interrogate him about his behaviour when her own had hardly been exemplary. By her keeping Santino's existence secret he had been presented with a baby, instead of having time to get used to the idea that he was to become a father.

Yet her pointed remark about his lack of interaction struck home, because what she said was true. He *had* kept his distance from Santino, telling himself that these things could not be rushed and needed time. And she had no right to demand anything of him, he thought bitterly. He would do things according to *his* agenda, not hers.

'Rome isn't far,' he said coolly. 'It is exactly two hundred kilometres. And I have a car constantly on standby.'

'Funnily enough that's something I *do* remember— being at your beck and call!'

'Then you will know there's no problem,' he said drily. 'Particularly as my driver is solid and reliable and not given to taking off to remote areas of the countryside in adverse weather conditions.'

'Very funny,' she said.

'We can be back here in an hour and a half should the need arise. We'll leave here at ten tomorrow morning—and be back early the next day. Less than twenty-four hours in the eternal city.' He gave a faintly cynical laugh. 'Don't women usually go weak at the knees at the prospect of an unlimited budget to spend on clothes?'

'Some women, maybe,' she said. 'Not me.'

But Keira's stubbornness was more than her determination not to become a rich man's doll. She didn't *know* about fashion—and the thought of what she might be expected to wear scared her. Perhaps if she'd been less of a tomboy, she might have flicked through glossy magazines like other women her age. She might have had some idea of what did and didn't suit her and would now be feeling a degree of excitement instead of dread. Fear suddenly became defiance and she glared at him.

'You are the bossiest man I've ever met!' she declared, pushing a handful of hair over her shoulder.

'And you are the most difficult woman I've ever encountered,' he countered. 'A little *gratitude* might go down well now and again.'

What, gratitude for his high-handedness and for making her feel stuff she'd rather not feel? Keira shook her head in frustration as she tugged her T-shirt down over her straining jeans.

'I'll be ready at ten,' she said, and went off to find Santino.

She put the baby in his smart new buggy to take him for a walk around the estate, slowly becoming aware that the weather had changed. The air had grown heavy and sultry and heavy clouds were beginning to accumulate on the horizon, like gathering troops. When eventually they returned to the farmhouse, Santino took longer than usual to settle for his sleep and Keira was feeling out of sorts when Paola came to ask whether she would be joining Signor Valenti for dinner that evening.

It was the first time she'd received such an invitation and Keira hesitated for a moment before declining. Up until now, she'd eaten her supper alone or with Claudia and she saw no reason to change that routine. She was going to be stuck with Matteo in Rome when clearly they were going to have to address some of the issues confronting them. Why waste conversation during a stilted dinner she had no desire to eat, especially when the atmosphere felt so close and heavy?

Fanning her face with her hand, she showered before bed but her skin still felt clammy, even after she'd towelled herself dry. Peering up into the sky, she thought she saw a distant flash of lightning through the thick curtain of clouds. She closed the shutters and brushed her hair before climbing into bed, but sleep stubbornly eluded her. She wished the occasional growl of thunder would produce the threatened rain and break some of the tension in the atmosphere and was just drifting off into an uneasy sleep when her wish came true. A loud clap of thunder echoed through the room and made her sit bolt upright in bed. There was a loud whoosh and heavy rain began to hurl down outside her window and quickly she got up and crept into Santino's room but, to her surprise, the baby was sound asleep.

How did he manage to do that? she thought enviously—feeling even more wide awake than before. She sighed as she went back to bed and the minutes ticked by, and all she could think about was how grim she was going to look, with dark shadowed eyes and a pasty face. Another clap of thunder made her decide that a warm drink might help relax her. And wasn't there a whole stack of herb teas in the kitchen?

To the loud tattoo of drumming rain, she crept downstairs to the kitchen with its big, old-fashioned range and lines of shiny copper pots hanging in a row. She switched on some low lighting and not for the first time found herself wistfully thinking how *homely* it looked—and how it was unlike any place she had imagined the urbane Matteo Valenti would own.

She had just made herself a cup of camomile tea when she heard a sound behind her and she jumped, her heart hammering as loudly as the rain as she turned to see Matteo standing framed in the doorway. He was wearing nothing but a pair of faded denims, which were clinging almost indecently to his long and muscular thighs. His mouth was unsmiling but there was a gleam in his coal-dark eyes, which made awareness drift uncomfortably over her skin and suddenly Keira began to shiver uncontrollably, her nipples tightening beneath her nightshirt.

CHAPTER SEVEN

THE WALLS SEEMED to close in on her and Keira was suddenly achingly conscious of being alone in the kitchen with a half-naked Matteo, while outside she could hear the rain howl down against the shuttered windows.

With a shaking hand she put her mug down, her eyes still irresistibly drawn to the faded jeans which hugged his long and muscular thighs. He must have pulled them on in a hurry because the top button was undone, displaying a line of dark hair which arrowed tantalisingly downwards. Soft light bathed his bare and gleaming torso, emphasising washboard abs and broad shoulders.

She realised with a start that she'd never seen his naked torso before—or at least hadn't really noticed it. She'd been so blown away when they'd been having sex that her eyes hadn't seemed able to focus on anything at all. But now she could see him in all his beauty— a dark and forbidding beauty, but beauty all the same. And despite all the *stuff* between them, despite the fact that they'd been snapping at each other like crocodiles this afternoon, she could feel herself responding to him, and there didn't seem to be a thing she could do about it.

Beneath her nightshirt her nipples were growing even tighter and her breasts were heavy. She could feel a warm melting tug at her groin and the sensation was so intense that she found herself shifting her weight uncomfortably from one bare foot to the other. She opened her mouth to say something, but no words came.

He stared at her, a strange and mocking half-smile at his lips, as if he knew exactly what was happening to her. 'What's the matter, Keira?' he queried silkily. 'Can't sleep?'

She struggled to find the correct response. To behave as anyone else would in the circumstances.

Like a woman drinking herb tea and not wishing that he would put his hand between her legs to stop this terrible aching.

'No. I can't. This wretched storm is keeping me awake.' She forced a smile. 'And neither could you, obviously.'

'I heard someone moving around in the kitchen, so I came to investigate.' He stared down at her empty cup. 'Is the tea working?'

She thought about pretending but what was the point? 'Not really,' she admitted as another crash of thunder echoed through the room. 'I'm still wide awake and I'm probably going to stay that way until the storm dies down.'

There was a pause while Matteo's gaze drifted over her and he thought how pale she looked standing there with her nightshirt brushing against her bare thighs and hair spilling like dark silk over her shoulders. Barefooted, she looked *tiny*—a tantalising mixture of vulnerability and promise—and it felt more potent than anything he'd ever experienced. She was trying to resist him, he knew that, yet the look in her eyes told him that inside she was aching as much as he was. He knew what he was going to do because he couldn't put it off any longer, and although the voice of his conscience was sounding loud in his ears, he took no notice of it. She needed to relax a little—for all their sakes.

'Maybe you should try a little distraction technique,' he said.

Her eyes narrowed. 'Doing what?'

'Come and look at the view from my study,' he suggested evenly. 'It's spectacular at the best of times, but during a storm it's unbelievable.'

Keira hesitated because it felt as if he were inviting her into the lion's lair, but surely anything would be better than standing there feeling totally out of her depth. What else was she going to do—go back to bed and lie there feeling sorry for herself? And they were leaving for Rome tomorrow. Perhaps she should drop her guard a little. Perhaps they should start trying to be friends.

'Sure,' she said, with a shrug. 'Why not?'

His study was in a different wing of the house, which hadn't featured in the guided tour he'd given her at the beginning of the week—an upstairs room sited at the far end of a vast, beamed sitting room. She followed him into the book-lined room, her introspection vanishing the instant she saw the light show taking place outside the window. Her lips fell open as she stood watching the sky blindingly illuminated by sheet lightning, which lit up the dark outlines of the surrounding mountains. Each bright flash was reflected in the surface of the distant lake, so that the dramatic effect of what she was seeing was doubled. 'It's...amazing,' she breathed.

'Isn't it?'

He had come to stand beside her—so close that he was almost touching and Keira held her breath, wanting him to touch her, *praying* for him to touch her. Did he guess that? Was that why he slid his arm around her shoulders, his fingers beginning to massage the tense and knotted muscles?

She looked up into the hard gleam of his eyes, startled by the dark look of hunger on his face.

'Shall we put a stop to all this right now, Keira?' he murmured. 'Because we both know that the damned storm has nothing to do with our inability to sleep. It's desire, isn't it? Two people lying in their lonely beds, just longing to reach out to one another.'

His hands had slipped to her upper arms, and as his hard-boned face swam in and out of focus Keira told herself to break away and escape to the sanctuary of her room. Yet her body was stubbornly refusing to obey. All she could seem to focus on were his lips and how good it felt to have him touching her like this. She'd never stood in a storm-lit room with a half-dressed man, completely naked beneath her frumpy nightshirt, and yet she knew exactly what was going to happen next. She could feel it. Smell it. She swayed. Could almost *taste* the desire which was bombarding her senses and making her pounding heart the only thing she could hear above the loud hammer of the rain.

'Isn't that so?' he continued, brushing hair away from

her face as the pad of his thumb stroked its way over her trembling lips. 'You want me to kiss you, don't you, Keira? You want it really quite badly.'

Keira resented the arrogance of that swaggering statement—but not enough to make her deny the truth behind it. 'Yes,' she said. 'Yes, I do.'

Matteo tensed, her whispered assent sharpening his already keen hunger, and he pulled her against his body and crushed his mouth over hers. And, oh, she tasted good. Better than good. Better than he remembered— but maybe that was because her kiss had lingered in his memory far longer than it should have done. He tried to go slowly but his usual patience fled as his hands began to rediscover her small and compact body. Before she had been incredibly lean—he remembered narrow hips and the bony ladder of her ribcage. But now those bones had disappeared beneath a layer of new flesh, which was soft and tempting and just ripe for licking.

Her head tipped back as he rucked up her nightshirt, his hand burrowing beneath the bunched cotton until he had bared her breast. He bent his head to take one taut rosebud in between his lips and felt her fingers digging into his bare shoulders as he grazed the sensitive are-ola between his teeth. Already he felt as if he wanted to explode—as if he would die if he'd didn't quickly impale her. Was the fact that she'd borne his child the reason why he was feeling a desire which felt almost *primitive* in its intensity? Was that why his hands were trembling like this?

'Do you know how long I've been wanting to do this?' he husked, his fingers sliding down between her breasts and caressing their silken weight. 'Every second of every day.'

Her reply was a muffled gasp against his mouth. 'Is that why you've stayed away from me?'

'That's exactly why.' He let his fingertips trickle down over her belly and heard her catch her breath as they travelled further downwards. 'You needed to rest and I was trying to be a...*gentleman*,' he growled.

'And how does this qualify as being...*oh*!' Her words faded away as he slid his hand between her legs, brushing over the soft fuzz of hair to find the molten heat beneath.

'You were saying?' he breathed as he dampened his finger in the soft, wet folds before starting to stroke the little bud which was already so tight.

He heard her give a shaky swallow. 'Matteo, this is...is...'

He knew exactly what it was. It was arousing her to a state where she was going to come any second, and while it was turning him on to discover how close to the edge she was—it was also making his own frustration threaten to implode. With a necessary care which defied his hungry impatience, he eased the zip of his jeans down over his straining hardness—breathing a sigh of relief as his massive erection sprang free. The denim concertinaed around his ankles but he didn't care. He knew propriety dictated he should take them off, but he couldn't. He couldn't wait, not a second longer.

Impatiently he pushed her back against his desk, shoving aside his computer and paperwork with uncharacteristic haste. And the moment the moist tip of his penis touched her, she seemed to go wild, clawing eagerly at his back—and it took more concentration than he'd ever needed to force himself to pull back. Through the distracting fog of desire, he recalled the condom concealed in a drawer of his desk and by the time it was in place he felt as excited as a teenage boy as his hungry gaze skated over her.

Like a sacrifice she lay on the desk, her arms stretched indolently above her head as he leaned over to make that first thrust deep inside her. And this time there was no pain or hesitation. This time there was nothing but a gasped cry of pleasure as he filled her. Greedily, he sank even deeper and then he rode her— and even the crash of something falling from the desk wasn't enough to put him off his stroke. Or maybe it was just another crash of thunder from the storm out- side. Who cared? He rode her until she came, her frantic convulsions starting only fractionally before his own, so that they moved in perfect time before his ragged groan heralded the end and he slumped on top of her, her hands clasped around the sweat-sheened skin of his back.

He didn't say anything at first, unwilling to shatter the unfamiliar peace he felt as he listened to the qui- etening of his heart. He felt spent. As if she had milked him dry. As if he could have fallen asleep right there, despite the hardness of the wooden surface. He forced himself to open his eyes and to take stock of their sur- roundings. Imagine if they were discovered here in the morning by one of the cleaners, or by Paola—already surprised that, not only had he brought a woman here, but he had a baby son.

A son he had barely seen.

Guilt formed itself into an icy-cold knot deep in his chest and was enough to dissolve his lethargy. Untwining himself from Keira's arms, he moved away from the desk, bending to pull up his jeans and zip them. Only then did he stare down at her, where she lay with her eyes closed amid the debris of his wrecked desk. Her cotton nightshirt was rucked right up to expose her beautiful breasts and her legs were bent with careless abandon. The enticing gleam between her open thighs was making him grow hard again but he fought the feeling—telling himself he needed to start taking control. He would learn about his son in time—he *would*—but for now his primary purpose was to ensure that Santino remained a part of his life, and for that to happen he needed Keira onside.

So couldn't their powerful sexual chemistry work in his favour—as effective a bargaining tool as his vast wealth? Couldn't he tantalise her with a taste of what could be hers, if only she was prepared to be reasonable? Because Keira Ryan was unpredictable. She was proud and stubborn, despite the fact that she'd been depending on other people's charity for most of her life, and he was by no means certain that she would accede to his wishes. So maybe it was time to remind her just who was calling the shots. He bent and lifted her into his arms, cradling her against his chest as her eyelashes fluttered open.

'What are you doing?' she questioned drowsily.

'Taking you back to bed.'

She yawned. 'Can't we just stay here?'

He gave an emphatic shake of his head. 'No.'

Keira closed her eyes again, wanting to capture this feeling for ever—a feeling which went much deeper than sexual satisfaction, incredible though that side of it had been. She had felt so close to Matteo when he'd been deep inside her. *Scarily* close—almost as if they were two parts of the same person. Had he felt that, too? Her heart gave a little leap of hope. Couldn't they somehow make this work despite everything which had happened? Couldn't they?

Resting her head against his warm chest, she let him carry her through the house to her own room, not pausing until he had pulled back the duvet and deposited her in the centre of the soft bed. Only then did her eyelids flutter open, her heart missing a beat as she took in his gleaming torso and powerful thighs. She stared up at him hopefully. Was he going to lose the jeans and climb in beside her, so she could snuggle up against him as she so desperately wanted to do and stroke her fingers through the ruffled beauty of his black hair?

She watched as his gaze swept over her, the hectic glitter of hunger in their ebony depths unmistakable. And she waited, because surely it should be *him* asking her permission to stay? She didn't know very much about bedroom etiquette, but instinct told her that. She recognised that she'd been a bit of a pushover back there, and it was time to show the Italian tycoon that he might need to work a little harder this time.

'So?' She looked at him with what she hoped was a welcoming smile.

'That's better. You don't smile nearly enough.' His finger traced the edges of her lips as he leaned over her. 'All the bad temper of this afternoon banished in the most pleasurable way possible.' He stroked an exploratory finger over the tightening nipple beneath her nightshirt. 'Was that what you needed all along, Keira?'

It took a few moments for his meaning to sink in and when it did, Keira could hardly believe her ears. A powerful wave of hurt crashed over her. Was that all it had been? Had he made love to her as a way of soothing her ruffled emotions and making her more *amenable*? As if he were some kind of *human sedative*? She wanted to bite down hard on her clenched fist. To demand how someone so cold-blooded could possibly live with himself. But she forced herself to remain silent because only that way could she cling onto what was left of her battered pride. Why give him the satisfaction of knowing he'd hurt her? If he was going to act so carelessly, then so would she. And why be so surprised by his callous behaviour when he hadn't shown one fraction of concern for his baby son. Matteo Valenti was nothing but a manipulative and cold-blooded *bastard*, she reminded herself.

Hauling the duvet up to her chin, she closed her eyes. 'I'm tired, Matteo,' she said. 'Would you mind turning off the light as you go?'

And then, deliberately manufacturing a loud yawn, she turned her back on him.

CHAPTER EIGHT

KEIRA DIDN'T SAY a word to Matteo next morning, not until they were halfway to Rome and his powerful car had covered many miles. The fierce storm had cleared the air and the day had dawned with a sky of clear, bright blue—but the atmosphere inside the car was heavy and fraught with tension. She was still feeling the painful tug of saying goodbye to Santino, though he'd been happily cradled in Claudia's arms when the dreaded moment had arrived. But as well as the prospect of missing her baby, Keira was still smarting from what had happened the night before.

She'd woken up with a start soon after dawn, wondering why her body felt so...

Slowly she had registered her lazy lethargy and the sweet aching between her legs.

So...*used.*

Yes, used, that was it. *Used.* Vivid images had flashed through her mind as she remembered what had happened while the storm raged outside. Matteo unzipping his jeans and pushing her onto his desk. Matteo rucking up her nightdress before thrusting into her and making her cry out with pleasure. It had hardly been the stuff of fairy tales, had it? So why not concentrate on the reality, rather than the dumb romantic version she'd talked herself into when she was lying quivering beneath his sweat-sheened body?

He had cold-bloodedly seduced her after days of acting as if she didn't exist. He had invited her to witness the storm from the best vantage point in the house and, although it had been the corniest request in the world, she had agreed. Trotting behind him like some kind of puppy dog, she'd had sex with him. Again. Keira closed her eyes in horror as she remembered the way she'd clawed at his bare back like some kind of wildcat. Did her inexperience explain the fierce hunger which had consumed her and made her unable to resist his advances? Or was it just that Matteo Valenti only had to touch her for her to come apart in his arms?

And now the trip to Rome, which she'd already been dreading, was going to be a whole lot worse. Bad enough being in the kind of car she'd lusted after during her days as a mechanic—and having it driven by *someone else*—without the knowledge of how smug Matteo must be feeling. Why, he hadn't even wanted to spend the night with her! He'd just deposited her in her bed like some unwanted package and behaved as if what had happened had been purely functional. Like somebody scratching an itch. Was that how it had been for him, she wondered bitterly? Had he seen her as a body rather than a person?

'So, are you going to spend the next twenty-four hours ignoring me?' Matteo's voice broke into her rebellious thoughts as they passed a signpost to a pretty-looking place called Civita Castellana.

Keira wanted to pretend she hadn't heard him but that was hardly the way forward, was it? She mightn't be happy with the current state of affairs, but that didn't mean she had to lie down and passively accept it. Unless she was planning on behaving like some sort of victim—allowing the powerful tycoon to pick her up and move her around at will, without her having any say in the matter. It was time she started asserting herself and stopped beating herself up. They'd had sex together as two consenting adults and surely that put them on some kind of equal footing.

So *ask* him.

Take some of the control back.

She turned her head to look at his profile, trying not to feel affected by that proud Roman nose and the strong curve of his shadowed jaw. His silk shirt was unbuttoned at the neck, offering a tantalising glimpse of olive skin, and he exuded a vitality which made him seem to glow with life. She could feel a trickle of awareness whispering over her body and it made her want to fidget on the plush leather car seat.

She wanted him to touch her all over again. And when he touched her she went to pieces.

Firmly pushing all erotic possibilities from her mind, she cleared her throat. 'So why this trip, Matteo?'

There was a pause. 'You know why. We've discussed this. We're going to buy you some pretty clothes to wear.'

His words were deeply patronising and she wondered

if that had been his intention—reminding her that she fell way short of his ideal of what a woman should be. 'I'm not talking about your determination to change my appearance,' she said. 'I mean, why bring me to Italy in the first place? That's something we haven't even discussed. What's going to happen once you've waved your magic wand and turned me into someone different? Are you planning to return me to England in your fancy plane and make like this was all some kind of dream?'

His mouth hardened into a flat and implacable line. 'That isn't an option.'

'Then what *are* the options?' she questioned quietly.

Matteo put his foot down on the accelerator and felt the powerful engine respond. It was a reasonable question, though not one he particularly wanted to answer. But he couldn't keep on putting off a conversation they needed to have because he was wary of all the stuff it might throw up. 'We need to see whether we can make it work as a couple.'

'A *couple*?'

He saw her slap her palms down on her denim-covered thighs in a gesture of frustration.

'You mean, living in separate parts of the same house? How is that in any way what a *couple* would do?' She sucked in a breath. 'Why, we've barely *seen* one another—and when we have, it isn't as if we've done much talking!'

'That can be worked on,' he said carefully.

'Then let's start working on it right now. Couples aren't complete strangers to one another and we are. Or at least, you are. I told you a lot about my circumstances on the night we…' Her voice wavered as she corrected herself before growing quieter. 'On that night we spent together in Devon. But I don't know you, Matteo. I still don't really know anything about you.'

Matteo stared at the road ahead. Women always asked these kinds of questions and usually he cut them short. With a deceptively airy sense of finality, he'd make it clear that he wouldn't tolerate any further interrogation because he didn't want anyone trying to 'understand' him. But he recognised that Keira was different and their situation was different. She was the mother of his child and she'd given birth to his heir—not some socially ambitious woman itching to get his ring on her finger. He owed her this.

'What do you want to know?' he questioned.

She shrugged. 'All the usual stuff. About your parents. Whether or not you have any brothers or sisters. That kind of thing.'

'I have a father and a stepmother. No siblings,' he said, his voice growing automatically harsher and there wasn't a damned thing he could do to stop it. 'But I have a stepbrother who's married, with a small child.'

He could feel her eyes on him. 'So your parents are divorced?'

'No. My mother is dead.'

'Like mine,' she said thoughtfully.

He nodded but didn't say anything, his attention fixed on the road ahead, trying to concentrate on the traffic and not on the bleak landscape of loss.

'Tell me about your father,' she said. 'Do you get on well with him?'

Some of the tension left his body as he overtook a truck and he waited until he had finished the manoeuvre before answering. He wondered if he should give her the official version of his life, thus maintaining the myth that all was well. But if she stayed then she would soon discover the undercurrents which surged beneath the surface of the powerful Valenti clan.

'We aren't close, no. We see each other from time to time, more out of duty than anything else.'

'But you mentioned a stepmother?'

'You mean the latest stepmother?' he questioned cynically. 'Number four in a long line of women who were brought in to try to replace the wife he lost.'

'But...' She hesitated. 'None of them were able to do that?'

'That depends on your definition. I'm sure each of them provided him with the creature comforts most men need, though each marriage ended acrimoniously and at great financial cost to him. That's the way it goes, I guess.' His hands tightened around the steering wheel. 'But my mother would have been a hard act for any woman to follow—at least according to the people who knew her.'

'What was she like?' she prompted, and her voice was as gentle as he'd ever imagined a voice could be.

Matteo didn't answer for a long time because this was something nobody ever really asked. A dead mother was just that. History. He couldn't remember anyone else who'd ever shown any interest in her short life.

He could feel the tight squeeze of his heart. 'She was beautiful,' he said eventually. 'Both inside and out. She was training to be a doctor when she met my father— an only child from a very traditional Umbrian family who owned a great estate in the region.'

'The farmhouse where we've been staying?' she questioned slowly. 'Is that...?'

He nodded. 'Was where she grew up, *sì*.'

Keira nodded as slowly she began to understand. She gazed out of the window at the blue bowl of the sky. Did that explain his obvious love for the estate? she wondered. The last earthly link to his mum?

'Does your father know?' she questioned suddenly. 'About Santino?'

'Nobody knows,' he said harshly. 'And I won't let it be known until we've come to some kind of united decision about the future.'

'But a baby isn't really the kind of thing you can keep secret. Won't someone from the farm have told him? One of the staff?'

He shook his head. 'Discretion is an essential quality for all the people who work for me and their first loyalty is to me. Anyway, my father isn't interested in the estate, only as...'

'Only as what?' she prompted, her curiosity sharpened by the harsh note which had suddenly entered his voice.

'Nothing. It doesn't matter. And I think we've had enough questions for today, don't you?' he drawled. He lifted one hand from the steering wheel to point straight ahead. 'We're skirting Rome now and if you look over there you'll soon be able to see Lake Nemi.'

Her gaze followed the direction of his finger as she tried to concentrate. 'And that's where you live?'

'That's where I live,' he agreed.

They didn't say much for the rest of the journey, but at least Keira felt she knew a little more about him. And yet it was only a little. He had the air of the enigma about him. Something at the very core of him which was dark and unknowable and which seemed to keep her at arm's length. Behind that formidable and sexy exterior lay a damaged man, she realised—and something about his inner darkness made her heart go out to him. *Could* they make it as a couple? she wondered as they drove through a beautiful sheltered valley and she saw the silver gleam of the lake. Would she be a fool to want that?

But the stupid thing was that, yes, she did want that, because if Santino was to have any kind of security— the kind she'd always longed for—then it would work best if they *were* a couple. Her living with Matteo Valenti as his lover and mother to his son…would that be such a bad thing?

Her daydreaming was cut short by her first sight of Matteo's villa and she began to wonder if she was crazy to ever imagine she would fit in here. Overlooking Lake Nemi, the apricot-coloured house was three storeys high, with high curved windows overlooking acres of beautifully tended gardens. And she soon discovered that inside were countless rooms, including a marble-floored dining room and a ballroom complete with a lavish hand-painted ceiling. It felt more like being shown round a museum than a house. Never had her coat felt more threadbare or the cuffs more frayed as it was plucked from her nerveless fingers by a stern-faced butler named Roberto, who seemed to regard her with complete indifference. Was he wondering why his powerful employer had brought such a scruffy woman to this palace of a place? Keira swallowed. Wasn't she wondering the same thing herself?

After ringing the farmhouse and being told by Paola that Santino was lying contentedly in his pram in the garden, Keira accepted the tiny cup of espresso offered by a maid in full uniform and sat down on a stiff and elegant chair to drink it. Trying to ignore the watchful darkness of Matteo's eyes, she found herself thinking about the relaxed comfort of the farmhouse and felt a pang as she thought about her son, wondering if he would be missing his mama. As she drank her coffee she found herself glancing around at the beautiful but cavernous room and suppressed a shiver, wondering how much it must cost to heat a place this size.

'Why do you live here?' she questioned suddenly, lifting her gaze to the dark figure of the man who stood beside the vast fireplace.

He narrowed his eyes. 'Why wouldn't I? It has a fresher climate than the city, particularly in the summer months when it can get very hot. And it's a valuable piece of real estate.'

'I don't doubt it.' She licked her lips. 'But it's *enormous* for just one person! Don't you rattle around in it?'

'I'm not a total hermit, Keira,' he said drily. 'Sometimes I work from here—and, of course, I entertain.'

The question sprang from her lips before she could stop it. 'And bring back loads of women, I expect?'

The look he shot her was mocking. 'Do you want me to create the illusion that I've been living a celibate life all these years?' he asked softly. 'If sexual jealousy was the reason behind your question?'

'It wasn't!' she denied, furious with herself for having asked it. Of *course* Matteo would have had hundreds of women streaming through these doors—and it wasn't as if he were her *boyfriend*, was it? Her cheeks grew red. He never had been. He was just a man who could make her melt with a single look, no matter how much she fought against it. A man who had impregnated her without meaning to. And now he was observing her with that sexy smile, as if he knew exactly what she was thinking. As if he was perfectly aware that beneath her drab, chain-store sweater her breasts were hungering to feel his mouth on them again. She could feel her cheeks growing warm as she watched him answer his mobile phone to speak in rapid Italian and when he'd terminated the call he turned to look at her, his hard black eyes scanning over her.

'The car is outside waiting to take you into the city centre,' he said. 'And the stylist will meet you there.'

'A stylist?' she echoed, her gaze flickering uncertainly to her scuffed brown boots.

'A very famous stylist who's going to take you shopping.' He shrugged. 'I thought you might need a little guidance.'

His condescension only intensified Keira's growing feelings of inadequacy and she glared at him. 'What, in case I opt for something which is deeply unsuitable?'

His voice was smooth. 'There is a different way of looking at it, Keira. I don't expect you've been given unlimited use of a credit card before, have you?'

Something in the way he said it was making Keira's blood boil. 'Funnily enough, no!'

'So what's the problem?'

'The problem is *you*! I bet you're just loving this,' she accused. 'Does flashing your wealth give you a feeling of power, Matteo?'

He raised his eyebrows. 'Actually, I was hoping it might give you a modicum of pleasure. So why don't you go upstairs and freshen up before the car takes you into the city?'

Keira put her empty cup down on a spindly gold-edged table and rose to her feet. 'Very well,' she said, forcing her stiff shoulders into a shrug.

'By the way,' he said as he gestured for her to precede him, 'I notice you didn't make any comment about my driving on the way here.'

'I thought it might be wise, in the circumstances.'

'But as a professional, you judged me favourably, I hope?'

She pursed her lips together. 'You were okay. A little heavy on the clutch, perhaps—but it's a great car.'

She took a stupid and disproportionate pleasure from the answering humour which gleamed from his eyes before following him up a sweeping staircase into a sumptuous suite furnished in rich brocades and velvets, where he left her. Alone in the ballroom-sized bathroom, where water gushed from golden taps, Keira dragged the hairbrush through her hair, wondering what on earth the stylist was going to think about being presented with such unpromising raw material.

But the stylist was upbeat and friendly—even if the store on the Via dei Condotti was slightly terrifying. Keira had never been inside such an expensive shop before—although in her chauffeuring days she'd sat outside places like it often enough, waiting for her clients. A slim-hipped woman named Leola came forward to greet her, dressed in an immaculate cream dress accessorised with gleaming golden jewellery and high-heeled patent shoes. Although she looked as if she'd stepped straight off the catwalk, to her credit, she didn't seem at all fazed by Keira's appearance, as she led her around the shop and swished her fingertips over rail after rail of clothes.

In the chandelier-lit changing room, she whipped a tape measure around Keira's newly abundant curves. 'You have a fantastic figure,' she purred. 'Let's show it off a little more, shall we?'

'I'd rather not, if you don't mind,' said Keira quickly. 'I don't like to be stared at.'

Leola raised perfectly plucked black eyebrows by a centimetre. 'You are dating one of the city's most eligible bachelors,' she observed quietly. 'And Matteo will expect people to stare at you.'

Keira felt a shimmer of anxiety as she tugged a blue cashmere dress over her head and pulled on some navy-blue suede boots. What possible response could she make to that? What would the stunning Leola say if she explained that she and Matteo weren't 'dating', but simply parents to a darling little boy? And even that wasn't really accurate, was it? You couldn't really describe a man as a parent when he regarded his newborn infant with the caution which an army expert might display towards an unexploded bomb.

Just go with the flow, she told herself. Be amenable and do what's suggested—and after you've been dressed up like a Christmas turkey, you can sit down with the Italian tycoon and talk seriously about the future.

She tried on hip-hugging skirts with filmy blouses, flirty little day dresses and sinuous evening gowns, and Keira was reeling by the time Leola had finished with her. She wanted to protest that there was no way she would wear most of these—that she and Matteo hadn't even discussed how long she would be staying—but Leola seemed to be acting on someone else's orders and it wasn't difficult to work out whose orders they might be.

'I will have new lingerie and more shoes sent by courier to arrive later,' the stylist explained, 'since I understand you're returning to Umbria tomorrow. But you certainly have enough to be going on with. Might I suggest you wear the red dress this evening? Matteo was very specific about how good he thought you would look in vibrant colours. Oh, and a make-up artist will be visiting the house later this afternoon. She will also be able to fix your hair.'

Keira stared at the slippery gown of silk-satin which was being dangled from Leola's finger and shook her head. 'I can do my own hair,' she said defensively, wondering if dressing up in all this finery was what Matteo usually expected for dinner at home on a weekday evening. 'And I can't possibly wear that—it's much too revealing.'

'Yes, you can—and you must—because you look amazing in it,' said Leola firmly, before her voice softened a little. 'Matteo must care for you a great deal to go to so much trouble. And surely it would be unwise to displease him when he's gone to so much trouble.'

It was a candid remark which contained in it a trace of warning. It was one woman saying to another—don't look a gift horse in the mouth. But all it did was to increase Keira's sensation of someone playing dress-up. Of being moulded for a role in the billionaire's life which she wasn't sure she was capable of filling. Her heart was pounding nervously as she shook the stylist's hand and went outside to the waiting car.

And didn't she feel slightly ashamed at the ease with which she allowed the chauffeur to open the door for her as she slid onto the squishy comfort of the back seat? As if already she was turning into someone she didn't recognise.

CHAPTER NINE

THE CLOCK WAS striking seven and Matteo gave a click of impatience as he paced the drawing room, where an enormous fire crackled and burned. Where the hell *was* she? He didn't like to be kept waiting—not by anyone, and especially not by a woman who ought to have been bang on time and full of gratitude for his generosity towards her. He wondered how long it would have taken Keira to discover how much she liked trying on lavish clothes. Or how quickly she'd decided it was a turn-on when a man was prepared to buy you an entire new wardrobe, with no expense spared. He was just about to send Roberto upstairs to remind her of the time, when the door opened and there she stood, pale-faced and slightly uncertain.

Matteo's heart pounded hard in his chest because she looked... He shook his head slightly as if to clear his vision, but the image didn't alter. She looked *unrecognisable*. Light curls of glossy black tumbled over her narrow shoulders and, with mascara and eyeliner, her sapphire eyes looked enormous. Her lips were as red as her dress and he found himself wanting to kiss away her unfamiliar lipstick. But it was her body which commanded the most attention. *Santo cielo!* What a body! Scarlet silk clung to the creamy curve of her breasts, the material gliding in over the indentation of her waist, then flaring gently over her hips. Sheer stockings encased her legs and skyscraper heels meant she looked much taller than usual.

He swallowed because the transformation was exactly what he'd wanted—a woman on his arm who would turn heads for all the *right* reasons—and yet now he was left with intense frustration pulsing through his veins. He wanted to call their host and cancel and to take her straight to bed instead, but he was aware that such a move would be unwise. He had less than twenty-four hours to get Keira Ryan to agree to his plan—and that would not be achieved by putting lust before logic.

'You look…beautiful,' he said unsteadily, noticing how pink her cheeks had grown in response to his compliment, and he was reminded once again of her innocence and inexperience.

She tugged at the skirt of the dress as if trying to lengthen it. 'I feel a bit underdressed, to be honest.'

He shook his head. 'If that were the case then I certainly wouldn't let you leave the house.'

She raised her eyebrows. 'What, you mean you'd keep me here by force? Prisoner of the Italian tycoon?'

He smiled. 'I've always found persuasion to be far more effective than force. I assume Leola organised a suitable coat for you to wear?'

'A coat?' She stared at him blankly.

'It's November, Keira, and we're going to a party in

the city. It might be warmer than back in England, but you'll still need to wrap up.'

Keira's stomach did a flip. 'You didn't mention a party.'

'Didn't I? Well, I'm mentioning it now.'

She gave the dress another tug. 'Whose party is it?'

'An old friend of mine. Salvatore di Luca. It's his birthday—and it will be the perfect opportunity for you to meet people. It would be a pity for you not to have an audience when you look so very dazzling.' His gaze travelled over her and his voice thickened. 'So why not go and get your coat? The car's waiting.'

Keira felt nerves wash over her. She was tempted to tell him she'd rather stay home and eat a *panino* in front of the fire, instead of having to face a roomful of strangers—but she was afraid of coming over as some kind of social misfit. Was this some strange kind of interview to assess whether or not she would be up to the task of being Matteo's partner? To see if she was capable of making conversation with his wealthy friends, of getting through a whole evening without dropping a canapé down the front of her dress?

Her black velvet swing coat was lined with softest cashmere and Keira hugged it around herself as the driver opened the door of the waiting limousine, her heart missing a beat as Matteo slid onto the seat beside her. His potent masculinity was almost as distracting as the dark suit which fitted his muscular body to perfection and made him look like some kind of movie star on his way to an awards ceremony. 'You aren't driving, then?' she observed.

'Not tonight. I have a few calls I need to make.' His black eyes gleamed. 'After that I'm exclusively yours.'

The way he said it sent ripples of excitement whispering over her skin and she wondered if that had been deliberate. But there was apprehension too because Keira wasn't sure she would be able to cope with the full blaze of his undivided attention. Not when he was being so... *nice* to her.

She suspected he was on his best behaviour because he wanted her to agree to his masterplan—whenever he got around to unveiling it. And although he hadn't shown any desire to parent their son, something told her that he saw Santino as his possession, even if so far he had exhibited no signs of love. Because of that, she suspected he wouldn't let her go easily and the stupid part was that she didn't want him to. She was beginning to recognise that she was out of her depth—and not just because he was a billionaire hotelier and she a one-time car mechanic. She didn't have any experience of relationships and she didn't have a clue how to react to him. Part of her wished she were still in the driver's seat, negotiating the roads with a slick professionalism she'd been proud of until she'd ruined her career in the arms of the man who sat beside her, his long legs stretched indolently in front of him.

She forced herself to drag her eyes away from the taut tension of his thighs—and at least there was plenty to distract her as she gazed out of the window at the lights of the city and the stunning Roman architecture, which made her feel as if she'd fallen straight into the pages of a guide book.

Salvatore de Luca's apartment was in the centre of it all—a penthouse situated close to the Via del Corso and offering commanding views of the city centre. Keira was dimly aware of a maid taking her coat and a cocktail being pressed into her hand and lots of people milling around. To her horror she could see that every other woman was wearing elegant black and her own expensive scarlet dress made her feel like something which had fallen off the Christmas tree. And it wasn't just the colour. She wasn't used to displaying a hint of cleavage, or wearing a dress which came this high above the knee. She felt like an imposter—someone who'd been more at home with her hair hidden beneath that peaked hat, instead of cascading over her shoulders like this.

She saw a couple of the men give her glances which lingered more than they should have done—or was that just something Italian men did automatically? Certainly, Matteo seemed to be watching her closely as he introduced her to a dizzying array of friends and she couldn't deny the thrill it gave her to feel those dark eyes following her every move.

Keira did her best to chat animatedly, hugely grateful that nearly everybody spoke perfect English, but conversation wasn't easy. She was glaringly aware of not mentioning the one subject which was embedded deeply in her heart and that was Santino. She wondered when Matteo was planning to announce that he was a father and what would happen when he did. Did any of his friends have children? she wondered. This apartment certainly didn't look child-friendly and she couldn't imagine a toddler crawling around on these priceless rugs, with sticky fingers.

Escaping from the growing pitch of noise to the washroom, Keira took advantage of the relative calm and began to peep into some of the rooms on her way back to the party. Entering only those with open doors, she discovered a bewildering number of hand-painted salons which reminded her of Matteo's villa. His home wasn't exactly child-friendly either, was it?

The room she liked best was small and book-lined—not because she was the world's greatest reader but because it opened out onto a lovely balcony with tall green plants in pots and fabulous views over the glittering city. She stood there for a moment with her arms resting on the balustrade when she heard the clip-clop of heels enter the room behind her and she turned to see a tall redhead who she hadn't noticed before. Maybe she was a late arrival, because she certainly wasn't the kind of woman you would forget in a hurry. Her green gaze was searching rather than friendly and Keira had to concentrate very hard not to be fixated on the row of emeralds which gleamed at her slender throat and matched her eyes perfectly.

'So *you're* the woman who's been keeping Matteo off the scene,' the woman said, her soft Italian accent making her sound like someone who could have a very lucrative career in radio voice-overs.

Keira left the chilly balcony and stepped into the room. 'Hello, I'm Keira.' She smiled. 'And you are?'

'Donatella.' Her green eyes narrowed, as if she was

surprised that Keira didn't already know this. 'Your
dress is very beautiful.'

'Thank you.'

There was a pause as Donatella's gaze flickered over
her. 'Everyone is curious to know how you've managed
to snare Italy's most elusive bachelor.'

'He's not a rabbit!' joked Keira.

Either Donatella didn't get the joke or she'd decided
it wasn't funny because she didn't smile. 'So when did
you two first meet?'

Aware of the sudden race of her heart, Keira suddenly felt *intimidated*. As if she was being backed into
a corner, only she didn't know why. 'Just under a year
ago.'

'When, exactly?' probed the redhead.

Keira wasn't the most experienced person when it
came to social etiquette, but even she could work out
when somebody was crossing the line. 'Does it really
matter?'

'I'm curious, that's all. It wouldn't happen to have
been two nights before Christmas, would it?'

The date was burned so vividly on Keira's memory
that the affirmation burst from her lips without her even
thinking about it. 'Yes, it was,' she said. 'How on earth
did you know that?'

'Because he was supposed to be meeting me that
night,' said Donatella, with a wry smile. 'And then I
got a call from his assistant to say his plane couldn't
take off because of the snow.'

'That's true. The weather was terrible,' said Keira.

'And then, when he got back—nothing. Complete

radio silence—even though the word was out that there was nobody else on the scene.' Donatella's green eyes narrowed thoughtfully. 'Interesting. You're not what I expected.'

Even though she hadn't eaten any of the canapés which had been doing the rounds, Keira suddenly felt sick. All she could think about was the fact that another woman had been waiting for Matteo while he'd been in bed with *her*. He must have had his assistant call Donatella while she'd been in the bath and then preceded to seduce *her*. Had it been a case of *any* woman would do as a recipient of all that hard hunger? A man who'd been intent on sex and was determined not to have his wishes thwarted? What if all that stuff about not finding her attractive had simply been the seasoned technique of an expert who'd recognised that he needed to get her to relax before leaping on her. She swallowed. Had he been imagining it was Donatella beneath him instead of her?

'Well, you know what they say…there's no accounting for taste.' From somewhere Keira dredged up a smile. 'Great meeting you, Donatella.'

But she was trembling by the time she located Matteo, surrounded by a group of men and women who were hanging onto his every word, and maybe he read something in her face because he instantly disengaged himself and came over to her side.

'Everything okay?' he questioned.

'Absolutely lovely,' she said brightly, for the benefit of the onlookers. 'But I'd like to go now, if you wouldn't mind. I'm awfully tired.'

His dark brows lifted. '*Certamente.* Come, let us slip away, *cara.*'

The practised ease with which the meaningless endearment fell from his lips made Donatella's words seem even more potent and in the car Keira sat as far away from him as possible, placing her finger on her lips and shaking her head when he tried to talk to her. She felt stupidly emotional and close to tears but there was no way she was going to break down in front of his driver. She knew better than most how domestic upsets could liven up a sometimes predictable job and that a chauffeur had a front-row seat to these kinds of drama. It wasn't until they were back in the villa, where a fire in the drawing room had obviously been kept banked for their return, that she turned to Matteo at last, trying to keep the edge of hysteria from her voice.

'I met Donatella,' she said.

'I wondered if you would. She arrived late.'

'I don't give a damn when she arrived!' She flung her sparkly scarlet clutch bag down onto a brocade sofa where it bounced against a tasselled cushion. 'She told me you were supposed to be meeting her the night we got stuck in the snow!'

'That much is true.'

She was so horrified by his easy agreement that Keira could barely choke out her next words. 'So you were in a sexual relationship with another woman when you seduced me?'

He shook his head. 'No, I was not. I'd been dating her for a few weeks, but it had never progressed beyond dinner and the occasional trip to the opera.'

'And you expect me to believe that?'

'Why wouldn't you believe it, Keira?'

'Because...' She sucked in a deep breath. 'Because you didn't strike me as the kind of man who would chastely court a woman like that.'

'Strangely enough, that's how I like to operate.'

'But not with me,' she said bitterly. 'Or maybe you just didn't think I was worth buying dinner for.'

Matteo tensed as he read the hurt and shame which clouded her sapphire eyes and was surprised how bad it made him feel. He knew he owed her an explanation but he sensed that this went deeper than anything he'd had to talk his way out of in the past, and part of him rebelled at having to lay his thoughts open. But he sensed there was no alternative. That despite the ease with which she had fallen into his arms, Keira Ryan was no pushover.

'Oh, you were worth it, all right,' he said softly. 'Just because we didn't do the conventional thing of having dinner doesn't change the fact that it was the most unforgettable night of my life.'

'Don't tell me lies!'

'It isn't a lie, Keira,' he said simply. 'It was amazing. We both know that.'

He saw her face working, as if she was struggling to contain her emotions.

'And then,' she said, on a gulp, 'when you got back— she says you didn't see her again.'

'Again, true.'

'Why not?' she demanded. 'There was nothing stopping you. Especially after you'd given me the heave-ho.'

If he was surprised by her persistence he didn't show it and Matteo felt conflicted about how far to go with his answer. Mightn't it be brutal to explain that he'd been so appalled at his recklessness that night that he'd decided he needed a break from women? If he told her that he'd never had a one-night stand before, because it went against everything he believed in, mightn't it hurt her more than was necessary? He didn't believe in love—not for him—but he believed in passion and, in his experience, it was always worth the wait. Deferred gratification increased the appetite and made seduction sweeter. And delaying his own pleasure reinforced his certainty that he was always in control.

Yet his usual fastidiousness had deserted him that snowy night when he'd found himself in bed with his petite driver, and it had affected him long after he'd returned to Italy. It wasn't an admission he particularly wanted to make but something told him it would work well in his favour if he did. What was it the Americans said? Ah, *sì*. It would buy him brownie points. 'I haven't had sex with anyone since the night I spent with you. Well, until last night,' he said.

Her eyes widened and the silence of the room was broken only by the loud ticking of the clock before she blurted out a single word.

'Why?' she breathed.

He bent to throw an unnecessary log onto the already blazing fire before straightening up to face the dazed disbelief which had darkened her eyes. He had tried convincing himself it had been self-disgust which had made him retreat into his shell when he'd returned to Rome, but deep down he'd known that wasn't the whole story.

'Because, annoyingly, I couldn't seem to shift you from my mind,' he drawled. 'And before you start shaking your head like that and telling me I don't mean it, let me assure you I do.'

'But why?' she questioned. 'I mean, why me?'

He paused long enough to let her know that he'd asked himself the same question. 'Who knows the subtle alchemy behind these things?' He shrugged, his gaze roving over her as he drank in the creamy curves of her flesh. 'Maybe because you were different. Because you spoke to me in a way that people usually don't. Or maybe because you were a virgin and on some subliminal level I understood that and it appealed to me. Why are you looking at me that way, Keira? You think that kind of thing doesn't matter? That a man doesn't feel an incomparable thrill of pleasure to discover that he is the first and the only one? Then you are very wrong.'

Keira felt faint and sank down onto the brocade sofa, next to her discarded clutch bag. His words were shockingly old-fashioned but that didn't lessen their impact on her, did it? It didn't stop her from feeling incredibly *desired* as his black gaze skated over her body and hinted at the things he might like to do to her.

Did her lips open of their own accord or did he somehow orchestrate her reaction from his position by the fireplace—like some puppet master twitching invisible strings? Was that why a hard gleam suddenly entered his eyes as he walked towards her and pulled her to her feet.

'I think we're done with talking, don't you?' he questioned unsteadily. 'Haven't I answered all your questions and told you everything you need to know?'

'Matteo, I—'

'I'm going to make love to you again,' he said, cutting right through her protest. 'Only this time it's going to be in a bed and it's going to be all night long. And please don't pretend you're outraged by the idea, when the look on your face says otherwise.'

'Or maybe you're just going to do it to pacify me?' she challenged. 'Like you did last night.'

'Last night we were in the middle of a howling storm and I wasn't really thinking straight, but today I am.'

And with that he lifted her up into his arms and swept her from the room and it occurred to Keira that no way would she have objected to such masterful treatment, even if he *had* given her the option. Because wasn't he making her feel like a woman who was completely desired—a woman for whom nothing but pleasure beckoned? Up the curving marble staircase he carried her, her ear pressed closely to his chest so she could hear the thundering of his heart. It felt like something from a film as he kicked the bedroom door shut behind them. Unreal. Just as the excitement coursing through her body felt unreal. Was it wrong to feel this rush of hungry pleasure as Matteo unzipped the scarlet dress and let it fall carelessly onto the silken rug? Or for her to gasp out words of encouragement from lips soon swollen by the pressure of his kiss?

Her bra swiftly followed and she gave a squeal of protesting pleasure as he hooked his fingers into the edges of her panties and ripped them apart and didn't that thrill her, too? Showing similar disregard for his own clothes, he tore them from his body like a man with the hounds of hell snapping at his ankles. But once they were both naked on the bed, he slowed things right down.

'These curves,' he said unevenly as his fingertips trickled over her breasts and hips.

'You don't like them?' she questioned breathlessly.

'Whatever gave you that idea? I seem to like you lean and I seem to like you rounded. Any way at all is okay with me, Keira.'

Slowly, he ran his fingertip from neck to belly before sliding it down between her thighs, nudging it lightly against her wet heat in a lazy and rhythmical movement. She shivered and had to stifle a frustrated moan as he moved his hand away. But then his mouth began to follow the same path as his fingers and Keira held her breath as she felt his lips acquainting themselves with the soft tangle of hair at her groin before he burrowed his head deep between her legs and made that first unbelievable flick of his tongue against her slick and heated flesh.

'Matteo!' she gasped, almost shooting off the bed with pleasure. 'What…what are you doing?'

He lifted his head and she saw pure devilry in his black eyes. 'I'm going to eat you, *cara mia*,' he purred, before bending his head to resume his task.

Keira let her head fall helplessly back against the pillow as he worked sweet magic with his tongue, loving the way he imprisoned her wriggling hips with the firm clamp of his hands. She came so quickly that it took her by surprise—as did the sudden way he moved over her to thrust deep inside her, while her body was still racked with those delicious spasms. She clung to his shoulders as he started a sweet, sure rhythm which set senses singing.

But suddenly his face hardened as he grew still inside her. 'How long do you think I can stop myself from coming?' he husked.

'Do you...?' She could barely get the words out when he was filling her like this. 'Do you *have* to stop yourself?'

'That depends. I do if you're going to have a second orgasm, which is my intention,' he murmured. 'In fact, I'm planning to make you come so often that you'll have lost count by the morning.'

'Oh, Matteo.' She closed her eyes as he levered himself to his knees and went even deeper.

She moaned as the finger moved between their joined bodies to alight on the tight nub between her legs and began to rub against her while he was deep inside her. The pleasure it gave her was almost too much to bear and it felt as if she were going to come apart at the seams. She gasped as pleasure and pressure combined in an unstoppable force. Until everything splintered around her. She heard him groan as his own body starting to convulse before eventually collapsing on top of her, his head resting on her shoulder and his shuddered breath hot and rapid against her neck.

His arms tightened around her waist and for countless seconds Keira felt as if she were floating on a cloud.

Had he really told her he hadn't slept with anyone else because he hadn't been able to get her out of his mind? Yes, he had. With a sigh of satisfaction, she rested her cheek against his shoulder and he murmured something soft in Italian in response.

She lay there for a long time after he'd fallen asleep, thinking that sex could blind you to the truth. Or maybe lull you into such a stupefied state that you stopped seeking the truth. He'd commented on her curves and admired them with his hands, but he'd made no mention of *why* her body had undergone such a dramatic transformation. She bit her lip. Because she'd carried his son and given birth to him—a fact he seemed to find all too easy to forget.

And she thought how—despite the heart-stopping intimacy of what had just taken place—she still didn't know Matteo at all.

CHAPTER TEN

She had to say something. She *had* to. She couldn't keep pretending nothing was wrong or that there weren't still a million questions buzzing around in her head which needed answering.

Keira turned her head to look at the face of the man who lay sleeping beside her. It was a very big bed, which was probably a good thing since Matteo Valenti's naked body was taking up most of it. Morning light flooded in from the two windows they hadn't bothered closing the shutters on before they'd tumbled into bed the night before. From here she could see the green of the landscape which spread far into the distance and, above it, the endless blue of the cloudless sky. It was the most perfect of mornings, following the most perfect of nights.

She hugged her arms around herself and gave a wriggle of satisfaction. She'd never thought she could feel the way Matteo had made her feel. But the clock was ticking away and she needed to face reality. She couldn't keep pretending everything was wonderful just because they'd spent an amazing night together. He'd said he wanted to explore the possibility of them becoming a couple but there was more to being a couple than amazing sex. How could they keep ignoring the gaping hole at the centre of their relationship which neither of them had addressed? He for reasons unknown and she...

She turned her attention from the distraction of the view to the dark head which lay sleeping beside her. Was she too scared to ask him, was that it?

Because the most important thing was all out of kilter and the longer it went on, the worse it seemed. Matteo acted as if Santino didn't exist. *As if he didn't have a son.* To her certain knowledge, he'd never even cuddled him—why, he'd barely even asked after him.

It didn't matter how many boxes the Italian ticked— she could never subject Santino to a life in which he was overlooked. And trying to compensate for his father's lack of regard with her own fierce love wouldn't work. She'd grown up in a house where she had been regarded as an imposition and no way was she going to impose that on her darling son.

Which left her with two choices. She could carry on being an ostrich and ignore what was happening—or rather, what wasn't happening. Or she could address the subject when Matteo woke and make him talk about it. She wouldn't accuse him or judge him. Whatever he told her, she would try to understand—because something told her that was very important.

Quietly, she slipped from the bed and went to the bathroom and when she returned with brushed teeth and hair, Matteo was awake—his black gaze following her as she walked back towards the bed.

'Morning,' she said shyly.

'Is this the point where I ask whether you slept well and you lower your eyelids and say, *not really*?' he murmured.

Blushing like a schoolgirl, Keira slipped rapidly beneath the covers so that her naked body was no longer in the spotlight of that disturbingly erotic stare. It was all very well being uninhibited when the room was in darkness but the bright morning light was making her feel awfully vulnerable. Especially as she sensed that Matteo wasn't going to like what she had to say, no matter how carefully she asked the question. He drew her into his arms but she gave him only the briefest of kisses before pulling her lips away. Because he needed to hear this, and the sooner, the better.

'Matteo,' she said, rubbing the tip of her finger over the shadowed angle of his jaw.

His brows knitted together. 'Why does my heart sink when you say my name that way?' he questioned softly.

She swallowed. 'You know we have to go back to Umbria soon.'

'You think I'd forgotten? Which is why I suggest we don't waste any of the time we have left.'

He had begun to stroke a light thumb over one of her nipples and although it puckered obediently beneath his touch, Keira pushed his hand away. 'And we need to talk,' she said firmly.

'And that was why my heart sank,' he drawled, shifting his body to lie against the bank of pillows and fixing her with a hooded look. 'Why do women always want to talk instead of making love?'

'Usually because something needs to be said.' She

pulled in a breath. 'I want to tell you about when I was growing up.'

The look on his face said it all. Wrong place; wrong time. 'I met your aunt,' he said impatiently. 'Over-strict guardian, small house, jealous cousin. I get it. You didn't have such a great time.'

Keira shook her head as uncomfortable thoughts flooded into her mind. She needed to be completely honest, else how could she expect complete honesty in return? Yet what she was about to tell him wasn't easy. She'd never told anyone the full story. Even her aunt. Especially her aunt. 'I told you my mother wasn't married and that I didn't know my father. What I didn't tell you was that she didn't know him either.'

His gaze was watchful now. 'What are you talking about?'

Keira flushed to the roots of her hair because she could remember her mother's shame when she'd finally blurted out the story, no longer able to evade the curious questions of her young daughter. Would her mother be appalled if she knew that Keira was now repeating the sorry tale, to a man with a trace of steel running through his veins?

'My mother was a student nurse,' she said slowly, 'who came to London and found it was nothing like the rural farm she'd grown up on in Ireland. She was quite shy and very naïve but she had those Irish looks. You know, black hair and blue eyes—'

'Like yours?' he interrupted softly.

She shook her head. 'Oh, no. She was much prettier than me. Men were always asking her out but usually she preferred to stay in the nurses' home and watch something on TV, until one night she gave in and went to a party with a group of the other nurses. It was a pretty wild party and not her kind of thing at all. People were getting wasted and Mum decided she didn't want to stay.' She swallowed. 'But by then it was too late because someone had...had...'

'Someone had what, Keira?' he questioned as her words became strangled and his voice was suddenly so gentle that it made her want to cry.

'Somebody spiked her drink,' she breathed, the words catching like sand in her throat because even now, they still had the power to repulse her. 'She...she woke up alone in a strange bed with a pain between her legs, and soon after that she discovered she was pregnant with me.'

He gave a terse exclamation and she thought he was going to turn away in disgust but to her surprise he reached out to push away the lock of hair which had fallen over her flushed cheeks, before slipping his hand round her shoulder and pulling her against the warmth of his chest. *'Bastardo,'* he swore softly and then repeated it, for added emphasis.

She shook her head and could feel the taste of tears nudging at the back of her throat and at last she gave into them, in a way she'd never done before. 'She didn't know how many men had been near her,' she sobbed. 'She had to go to the clinic to check she hadn't been given some sort of disease and of course they offered her...' She swallowed away the tears because she saw from the tightening of his jaw that she didn't actually need to spell it out for him. 'But she didn't want that. She wanted me,' she said simply. 'There wasn't a moment of doubt about that.'

He waited until she had composed herself before he spoke again, until she had brushed the remaining tears away with the tips of her fingers.

'Why are you telling me all this, Keira?' he questioned softly. 'And why now?'

'Because I grew up without a father and for me there was no other option—but I don't want the same for my baby. For… Santino.' Her voice wavered as she looked into the hardness of his eyes and forced herself to continue, even though the look on his face would have intimidated stronger people than her. 'Matteo, you don't… you don't seem to feel anything for your son.' She sucked in a deep breath. 'Why, you've barely *touched* him. It's as if you can't bear to go near him and I want to try to understand why.'

Matteo released his hold on her and his body tensed because she had no right to interrogate him, and he didn't *have* to answer her intrusive question. He could tell her to mind her own damned business and that he would interact with his son when he was good and ready and not according to *her* timetable. Just because she wanted to spill out stuff about her own past, didn't mean he had to do the same, did it? But in the depths of her eyes he could read a deep compassion and something in him told him there could be no going forward unless she understood what had made him the man he was.

He could feel a bitter taste coating his throat. Maybe everyone kept stuff hidden away inside them—the stuff which was truly painful. Perhaps it was nature's way of trying to protect you from revisiting places which were too dark to contemplate. 'My mother died in childbirth,' he said suddenly.

There was a disbelieving pause as the words sank in and when they did, her eyes widened. 'Oh, Matteo. That's terrible,' she whispered.

Matteo instantly produced the self-protective clause which enabled him to bat off unwanted sympathy if people *did* find out. 'What is it they say?' He shrugged. 'That you can't miss what you've never had. And I've had thirty-four years to get used to it.'

Her muffled 'But...' suggested she was about to disagree with him, but then she seemed to change her mind and said nothing. Leaving him free to utter the next words from his set-piece statement. 'Maternal death is thankfully rare,' he bit out. 'My mother was just one of the unlucky ones.'

'I'm so sorry.'

'Yes,' he said. 'I think we've established that.' He chose his words carefully. 'I've never come into contact with babies before. To be honest, I've never even held one, but you're right—it isn't just inexperience which makes me wary.' His jaw tightened. 'It's guilt.'

'Guilt?' she echoed, in surprise.

He swallowed and the words took a long time in coming. 'People say they feel instant love for their own child but that didn't happen to me when I looked at Santino for the first time. Oh, I checked his fingers and his toes and was relieved that he was healthy, but I didn't *feel* anything.' He punched his fist against his heart and the words fell from his lips, heavy as stones. 'And I don't know if I ever can.'

Keira nodded as she tried to evaluate what he'd told her. It all made sense now. It explained why he'd thrown a complete wobbly when she'd kept her pregnancy quiet. What if history had grimly repeated itself and she'd died in childbirth as his mother had done? Nobody had known who the father of her baby was because she'd kept it secret. Wasn't it possible that Santino could have been adopted by her aunt and her cousin and grown up without knowing anything of his roots?

She felt another wrench as she met the pain in his eyes. What must it have been like for him—this powerful man who had missed out on so much? He had never experienced a mother's love. Never even felt her arms hugging him in those vital hours of bonding which followed birth. Who had cradled the tiny Matteo as the cold corpse of his mother was prepared for her silent journey to the grave, instead of a joyous homecoming with her newborn baby? No wonder he'd been so reluctant to get close to his little boy—he didn't know *how*.

'Didn't your father make up for the fact that you didn't have a mother?'

His mouth twisted and he gave a hollow laugh. 'People cope in their own way—or they don't. He left my care to a series of young nannies, most of whom he apparently slept with—so then they'd leave—or the new stepmother would fire them. But it didn't seem to matter how much sex he had or how many women he married, he never really got over my mother's death. It left a hole in his life which nothing could ever fill.'

Keira couldn't take her eyes away from his ravaged face. Had his father unconsciously blamed his infant son for the tragic demise of his beloved wife—would that explain why they weren't close? And had Matteo been angry with his father for trying to replace her? She wondered if those different stepmothers had blamed the boy for being an ever-present reminder of a woman they could never compete with.

And blame was the last thing Matteo needed, Keira realised. Not then and certainly not now. He needed understanding—and love—though she wasn't sure he wanted either. Reaching out, she laid her hand on his bunched and tensed biceps but the muscle remained hard and stone-like beneath her fingers. Undeterred, she began to massage her fingertips against the un-yielding flesh.

'So what do we do next, now we've brought all our ghosts into the daylight?' she questioned slowly. 'Where do we go from here, Matteo?'

His gaze was steady as he rolled away from her touch, as if reminding her that this was a decision which needed to be made without the distraction of the senses. 'That depends. Where do you want to go from here?'

She recognised he was being open to negotiation and on some deeper level she suspected that this wasn't usual for him in relationships. Because this *was* a relationship, she realised. Somehow it had grown despite their wariness and private pain and the unpromising beginning. It had the potential to grow even more—but only if she had the courage to give him the affection he needed, without making any demands of her own in return. She couldn't *demand* that he learn to love his son, she could only pray that he would. Just as she couldn't demand that he learn to love *her*. 'I'll go anywhere,' she whispered. 'As long as it's with Santino. And you.'

She leaned forward to kiss him and Matteo could never remember being kissed like that before. A kiss not fuelled by sexual hunger but filled with the promise of something he didn't recognise, something which started his senses humming. He murmured something in objection when she pulled back a little, her eyes of *profondo blu* looking dark and serious, but at least when she wasn't kissing him he was able to think straight. He didn't understand the way she made him feel, but maybe that didn't matter. Because weren't the successes of life—and business—based on gut feeling as much as understanding? Hadn't he sometimes bought a hotel site even though others in the business had told him he was crazy—and turned it into a glittering success because deep down he'd known he was onto a winner? And wasn't it a bit like that now?

'I will learn to interact with my son,' he said.

'That's a start,' she said hesitantly.

The look on her face suggested that his answer had fallen short of the ideal—but he was damned if he was going to promise to love his son. Because what if he failed to deliver? What if the ice around his heart was so deep and so frozen that nothing could ever penetrate it? 'And I want to marry you,' he said suddenly.

Now the look on her face had changed. He saw surprise there and perhaps the faint glimmer of delight, which was quickly replaced by one of suspicion, as if perhaps she had misheard him.

'Marry me?' she echoed softly.

He nodded. 'So that Santino will have the security you never had, even if our relationship doesn't last,' he said, his voice cool but certain. 'And so that he will be protected by my fortune, which one day he will inherit. Doesn't that make perfect sense to you?'

He could see her blinking furiously, as if she was trying very hard to hold back the glitter of disappointed tears, but then she seemed to pull it all together and nodded.

'Yes, I think marriage is probably the most sensible option in the circumstances,' she said.

'So you will be my wife?'

'Yes, I'll be your wife. But I'm only doing this for Santino. To give him the legitimacy I never had. You do understand that, don't you, Matteo?'

She fixed him with a defiant look, as if she didn't really care—and for a split second it occurred to him that neither of them were being completely honest. 'Of course I understand, *cara mia*,' he said softly.

CHAPTER ELEVEN

KEIRA HEARD FOOTSTEPS behind her and turned from the mirror to see Claudia in a pretty flowery dress, instead of the soft blue uniform she usually wore when she was working.

'Is everything okay with Santino?' Keira asked the nursery nurse immediately, more out of habit than fear because she'd been cradling him not an hour earlier as she had dressed her baby son in preparation for his parents' forthcoming marriage.

Claudia smiled. 'He is well, *signorina*. His father is playing with him now. He says he is teaching him simple words of Italian, which he is certain he will remember when eventually he starts to speak.'

Keira smiled, turning back to her reflection and forcing herself to make a final adjustment to her hair, even though she kept telling herself that her bridal outfit was pretty irrelevant on what was going to be a purely functional wedding day. But Matteo's father and stepmother were going to be attending the brief ceremony, so she felt she had to make *some* sort of effort. And surely if she did her best it might lessen their inevitable disbelief that he was going to marry some-one like her.

'What kind of wedding would you like?' Matteo had asked during that drive back from Rome after she'd agreed to be his wife.

Keira remembered hedging her bets. 'You first.'

She remembered his cynical laugh, too.

'Something small. Unfussy. I'm not a big fan of wed-dings.'

So of course Keira had agreed that small and un-fussy would be perfect, though deep down that hadn't been what she'd wanted at all. Maybe there was a part of every woman which wanted the whole works—the fuss and flowers and clouds of confetti. Or maybe that was just her—because marriage had always been held up as the perfect ideal when she'd been growing up. There had been that photo adorning her aunt's side-board—the bouquet-clutching image which had stared out at her over the years. She recalled visiting for Sun-day tea when her mother was still alive, when attention would be drawn to Aunt Ida's white dress and stiff veil. 'Wouldn't you have loved a white wedding, Bridie?' Ida used to sigh, and Keira's mother would say she didn't care for pomp and ceremony.

And Keira had thought she was the same—until she'd agreed to marry Matteo and been surprised by the stupid ache in her heart as she realised she must play down a wedding which wasn't really a wedding. It was a legal contract for the benefit of their son—not some-thing inspired by love or devotion or a burning desire to want to spend the rest of your life with just one person, so it didn't really count. At least, not on Matteo's part.

And hers?

She smoothed down her jacket and sighed. Because even more disturbing than her sudden yearning to wear a long white dress and carry a fragrant bouquet was the realisation that her feelings for Matteo had started to change. Was that because she understood him a little better now? Because he'd given her a glimpse of the vulnerability and loss which lay beneath the steely exterior he presented to the world? Maybe. She told herself not to have unrealistic expectations. Not to wish for things which were never going to happen, but concentrate on being a good partner. To give Matteo affection in quiet and unobtrusive ways, so that maybe the hard ice around his heart might melt a little and let her in.

He was doing his best to change, she knew that. In the busy days which followed their return from his Roman villa, he had meticulously paid his son all the attention which had been lacking before. Sometimes he would go to Santino if he woke in the night—silencing Keira's sleepy protests with a kiss. Occasionally, he gave the baby a bottle and, once, had even changed his nappy, even though he'd protested that this was one task surely better undertaken by women.

But as Keira had watched him perform these fatherly duties she had been unable to blind herself to the truth. That it *was* simply a performance and Matteo was just going through the motions. He was being a good father, just as he was a good lover—because he was a man who excelled in whatever he did. But it was duty which motivated him. His heart wasn't in it, that much was obvious. And as long as she accepted that, then she'd be fine.

She turned away from the mirror, wondering if there was anything she'd forgotten to do. Matteo's father, Massimo, and his wife, Luciana, had arrived only a short while ago because the traffic from Rome had been bad. Since they were due at the town hall at noon, there had been little opportunity for Keira to exchange more than a few words of greeting and introduce them to their new grandson. She'd been nervous—of course she had—she suspected it was always nerve-racking meeting prospective in-laws, and most people didn't have to do it on the morning of the wedding itself.

Massimo was a bear of a man, his build bulkier than Matteo's, though Keira could see a likeness around the jet-dark eyes. Her prospective stepmother-in-law, Luciana, was an elegant woman in her fifties, who had clearly embraced everything facial surgery had to offer, which had resulted in a disturbingly youthful appearance.

Keira picked up her clutch bag and went downstairs, her heart pounding with an anxiety which seemed to be increasing by the second. Was that because she'd seen Luciana's unmistakable look of disbelief when they'd been introduced? Was she wondering how this little Englishwoman from nowhere had wrested a proposal of marriage from the Italian tycoon?

But the expression on Matteo's face made Keira's stomach melt as she walked into the hallway, where everyone was waiting. She saw his eyes darken and the edges of his lips curve into an unmistakable smile of appreciation as he took her cold hand in his and kissed it.

'*Sei bella, mia cara,*' he had murmured softly. '*Molta bella.*'

Keira told herself he was only saying it because such praise was expected of the prospective groom, but she couldn't deny the feeling of satisfaction which rippled down her spine in response. Because she *wanted* him to look at her and find her beautiful, of course she did. She wasn't stupid and knew she couldn't take his desire for granted. Someone like her was always going to have to work to maintain it. Leola the stylist had been dispatched from Rome with a selection of wedding outfits and Keira had chosen the one she felt was the most flattering but also the most *appropriate*. Steadfastly pushing away the more floaty white concoctions, she had opted for functional rather than fairy tale. The silvery-grey material of the dress and jacket reminded her of a frosty winter morning but there was no doubt that it suited her dark hair and colouring. Only the turquoise shoes and matching clutch bag provided a splash of colour—because she had refused all Leola's inducements to carry flowers.

At least Massimo Valenti seemed enchanted by his grandson. Keira travelled in one of the cars with him to the nearly town and watched as he spent the entire journey cooing at the baby in delight. It made her wonder why he hadn't been close to his own son—but there was no time for questions because they were drawing up outside the town hall where Matteo was waiting to introduce her to the interpreter, which Italian law demanded.

Twenty minutes later she emerged from the building as a married woman and Matteo was pulling her into his arms, his hands resting on either side of her waist—but even that light touch was enough to make her want to dissolve with lust and longing.

'So. How does it feel to be Signora Valenti?' he questioned silkily.

Her heart was pounding as she stared up into the molten darkness of his eyes. 'Ask me again next week,' she said breathlessly. 'It feels a little unreal right now.'

'Maybe this will help you accept the reality,' he said, *'mia sposa.'*

And there, beneath the fluttering Italian flag of the town hall, his lips came down to claim hers with a kiss which left her in no doubt that he would rather they were somewhere private, preferably naked and horizontal. It set off an answering hunger and reminded Keira of the slightly incredible fact that he couldn't seem to get enough of her. Didn't he demonstrate that every night when he covered her trembling body with his own? And wasn't that *enough?* she wondered as they drove back to the farmhouse together, her golden ring glinting as she fussed around with Santino's delicate shawl. Was it just her inherently cautious nature which made her wonder if her relationship with Matteo was as superficial as the icing sugar sprinkled over the top of the chocolate wedding cake which Paola had baked?

Yet when he carried her over the threshold, it felt real. And when she returned from putting Santino down

for a nap, having removed the silvery-grey jacket to reveal the filmy chiffon dress beneath, Matteo had been
waiting in the shadowed hallway for her.

Pulling her into a quiet alcove, he placed his palm
over her hammering heart and she licked her lips as
her nipple automatically hardened beneath his touch.

'Ever wish you could just wave a magic wand and
make everyone disappear?' he drawled.

She shivered as the light stroking of her nipple increased. 'Isn't that a little…anti-social?'

'I'm feeling anti-social,' he grumbled, his lips brushing over the curve of her jaw before moving upwards to
tease her now trembling lips. 'I want to be alone with
my new wife.'

Keira kissed him back as his words set off another
whisper of hope inside her and she wondered if it was
wrong to allow herself to hope, on this, her wedding
day.

'You were the man who once told me about the ben-
efits of waiting,' she teased him. 'Won't this allow you
to test out your theory?'

Matteo laughed as she pulled away from him, the
prim twitch of her lips contradicting the hunger in her
eyes, and he shook his head slightly, wondering what
kind of spell she had cast over him. He was used to the
wiles of women yet Keira used none of them. She wasn't
deliberately provocative around him and didn't possess
that air of vanity of someone who revelled in her sexual
power over a man. On the contrary, in public she was
almost demure—while in private she was red-hot. And
that pleased him, too. She pleased him and unsettled

him in equal measure. She left him wanting more—but more of *what*, he didn't know. She was like a drink you took when your throat was dry yet when you'd finished it, you found that your thirst was just as intense.

He stroked his fingers down over her belly, his gaze steady as they stood hidden by the shadows of the staircase. Hard to believe that a child had grown beneath its almost-flat curve. 'I want you to know you are an amazing mother,' he said suddenly. 'And that Santino is blessed indeed.'

He saw the surprise behind the sudden brightness in her eyes, her mouth working as she struggled to contain herself.

'Don't make me get all emotional, Matteo,' she whispered. 'I've got to go in there and make conversation with your father and stepmother and I'm not going to make a very good impression if I've been blubbing.'

But he disregarded her soft plea, knowing he needed to express something which had slowly become a certainty. He owed her that, at least. 'I shouldn't have taken you to Rome when I did and made you leave the baby behind,' he admitted slowly. 'No matter how good the childcare we had in place. I can see now that it was a big ask for a relatively new mother in a strange country.'

He saw her teeth working into her bottom lip and he thought she might be about to cry, when suddenly she smiled and it was like the bright summer sun blazing all over him with warmth and light, even though outside it was cold and wintry.

'Thank you,' she said, a little shakily. 'I love you for saying that.'

He stilled. 'Really?'

A look of horror crossed her face as she realised what she'd said. 'I didn't mean—'

'Didn't you?' he murmured. 'How very disappointing.'

Keira told herself he was only teasing as he led her into the salon, but she felt as if she were floating on air as she took a grizzling Santino from Massimo's bear-like arms and rocked him dreamily against her chest. Had Matteo really just admitted he'd been in the wrong by taking her to Rome and told her she was a good mother? It wasn't so much the admission itself, more the fact he was beginning to accept that each and every one of them got it wrong sometimes—and that felt like a major breakthrough.

And had she really just let her guard down enough to tell him she loved him? It hadn't been in a dramatic way or because she'd expected an instant reciprocal response. She'd said it affectionately and Matteo needed that, she reckoned. How many times had he been told he'd been loved when he was growing up? Too few, she suspected.

Still high from the impact of their conversation, Keira refused the glass of vintage champagne which was offered and accepted a glass of some bittersweet orange drink instead.

But unusually, Santino grizzled in her arms and she wondered if it was the excitement of the day which was making him so fractious. Discreetly, she slipped away to the nursery to feed and change him before rocking him until he was sound asleep and carefully putting him in his crib.

She picked up the empty bottle and was just on her way out when she was startled by the sight of Luciana, who suddenly appeared at the nursery door in a waft of expensive scent. Keira wondered if she'd wandered into the wrong room or if she'd been hoping for a cuddle with Santino. But there was an odd smile on her new stepmother's face and, for some reason, whispers of trepidation began to slide over Keira's spine.

'Is everything okay, Luciana?' she questioned, hoping she sounded suitably deferential towards the older woman.

Luciana shrugged. 'That depends what you mean by *okay*. I was a little disappointed that my son and his family were not invited to the ceremony today.'

'Oh, well—you can see how it is.' Keira gave a nervous smile, because Matteo had hinted that there was no love lost between him and his stepbrother, Emilio. 'We just wanted a very small wedding.'

'*Sì.*' Luciana picked up a silver-framed photo of Santino and began to study it. 'And naturally, it would have been very *difficult* for Emilio.'

'Difficult?'

Luciana put the photograph down. 'In the circumstances.'

Keira blinked. 'What circumstances?'

Elegantly plucked eyebrows were raised. 'Because of the clause in my husband's will, of course.'

Keira's heart began to pound as some nameless dread crept over her. 'What clause?'

'Surely Matteo has told you?' Luciana looked surprised. 'Though perhaps not. He has always been a man who gives very little away.' Her expression became sly. 'You are aware that this house belonged to Massimo's first wife?'

'To Matteo's mother?' questioned Keira stiffly. 'Yes, I knew that. It's where she was born and where she grew up. It's one of the reasons he loves it so much.'

Luciana shrugged. 'Ever since Matteo reached the age of eighteen, Massimo has generously allowed his son to use the estate as his own. To all intents and purposes, this *was* Matteo's home.' She paused. 'But a strange thing happens to men as they grow older. They want to leave something of themselves behind.' Her surgically enhanced eyes gleamed. 'I'm talking, of course, about continuing the Valenti name. I am already a grandmother. I understand these desires.'

Keira's head was spinning. 'I honestly don't understand what you're getting at, Luciana.'

'Ah, I can see you know nothing of this.' Luciana gave a hard smile. 'It's very simple. He loves this house for obvious reasons, but he does not *own* it. And Massimo told him he intended bequeathing the entire estate to his stepson, unless Matteo produced an heir of his own with the Valenti name.' She shrugged her bony shoulders. 'I wondered if he would be prepared to sacrifice his freedom for an heir, not least because he has always shown a certain...*disdain* for women. And yet here you are—a pretty little English girl who arrived with a baby in her arms and got a wedding ring for her troubles. The perfect solution to all Matteo's problems!'

'You're saying that...that Matteo would have lost this house unless he produced an heir?'

'That's exactly what I'm saying. His gain, my son's loss.' Luciana shrugged. *'C'est la vie.'*

Keira felt so shocked that for a moment her limbs felt as if they were completely weightless. With a shaking hand, she put the empty bottle down on a shelf and swallowed, trying to compose herself—and knowing that she had to get away from Luciana's toxic company before she did or said something she regretted. 'Please excuse me,' she said. 'But I must get back to the wedding party.'

Did she imagine the look of disappointment which flickered across Luciana's face, or did she just imagine it? It didn't matter. She was going to get through this day with her dignity intact. Matteo had married her to get his hands on this property, so let him enjoy his brief victory. What good would come of making a scene on her wedding day?

Somehow she got through the rest of the afternoon, meeting Matteo's questioning stare with a brittle smile across the dining table, while everyone except her tucked into the lavish wedding breakfast. Did he sense that all was not well, and was that the reason why his black gaze seemed fixed on her face?

She was relieved when finally Massimo and Luciana left—though her father-in-law gave her the most enormous hug, which brought an unexpected lump to her throat. Leaving Matteo to dismiss Paola and the rest of the staff, Keira hurried to tend to Santino, spending far longer than necessary as she settled her baby son for the night.

At last she left the nursery and went into the bedroom but her hands were clammy as she pulled off her wedding outfit and flung it over a chair. Spurred on by Leola, she had been planning on surprising Matteo with the shortest dress she'd ever worn. A bottom-skimming dress for his eyes and no one else's. She'd wanted to wear it in anticipation of the appreciative look on his face when he saw it and to hint at a final farewell to her residual tomboy. But now she tugged on a functional pair of jeans and a sweater because she couldn't bear the thought of dressing up—not when Matteo's motives for marrying her were making her feel so *ugly* inside.

Although she would have liked nothing better than to creep into bed on her own and pull the duvet over her head to blot out the world, she knew that wasn't an option. There was only one acceptable course of action which lay open to her, but she couldn't deny her feeling of dread as she walked into the room which overlooked the garden at the back of the house, where Matteo stood beside the fire, looking impossibly handsome in his charcoal wedding suit. Don't touch me, she prayed silently, even though her body desperately wanted him to do just that—and maybe something had alerted him to her conflicted mood because his eyes narrowed and he made no attempt to approach her.

His face was sombre as he regarded her. 'Something is wrong.'

It was a statement, not a question, but Keira didn't answer straight away. She allowed herself a few more seconds before everything changed for ever. A final few seconds where she could pretend they were newlyweds about to embark on a shared life together. 'You could say that. I had a very interesting conversation with Luciana earlier.' She inhaled deeply and then suddenly the words came spilling out, like corrosive acid leaking from a car battery. 'Why didn't you tell me you were only marrying me to get your hands on an inheritance?' she demanded. 'And that this house would only become yours if you produced a legitimate child? I would have understood, if only you'd had the guts to tell me.'

He didn't flinch. His gaze was hard and steady. 'Because the inheritance became irrelevant. I married you because I care for you and my son and because I want us to make a future together.'

Keira wanted to believe him. The child-woman who had yearned for a long white dress and big bouquet of flowers longed for it to be the truth. But she couldn't believe him—it was a stretch too far. Once she'd thought he sounded like someone reading from a script when he'd been addressing a subject which would make most people emotional—and he was doing it again now.

I care for you and my son.

He sounded like a robot intoning the correct response, not someone speaking from the heart. And his lack of emotion wasn't the point, was it? She'd known about that from the start. She'd known the reason he was made that way and, filled with hope and with trust, had been prepared to make allowances for it. She bit her lip. When all the time he'd been plotting away and using her as a pawn in his desire to get his hands on this estate.

'I understand that you're known as an elusive man who doesn't give anything away,' she accused shakily. 'But how many more people are going to come out of the woodwork and tell me things about you that I didn't know? Can you imagine how it made me feel to hear that from Luciana, Matteo? To know you'd been buttering me up to get me to marry you? I thought... I thought you were doing it for your son's future, when all the time it was because you didn't want to lose a piece of land you thought of as rightfully yours! You don't want a family—not really—you've just used me as some kind of incubator!'

'But there's a fundamental flaw in your argument,' he grated. 'If inheriting the estate meant so much to me, then why hadn't I fathered a child with someone else long before I met you?'

'Because I don't think you really like women,' she said slowly. 'Or maybe you just don't understand them. You never knew your mother and she died so tragically that it's inevitable you idealised her. She would have had flaws, just like we all do—only you never got to see them. No woman could ever have lived up to her and maybe that's one of the reasons why you never settled down.' She sucked in a deep breath. 'And then I came along and took the decision away from you. A stolen night, which was never meant to be any more, suddenly produced an heir. You didn't have to go through the whole tedious ritual of courting a woman you didn't care for in order to get yourself a child. Fate played right into your hands, didn't it, Matteo? Suddenly you had everything you needed, without any real effort on your part.'

His face blanched. 'You think I am so utterly ruthless?'

She shrugged. 'I don't know,' she said, and there was

a crack in her voice. 'Maybe you do care—a little. Or as much as you ever can. But you're missing the point. I thought growing up without a father was difficult, but at least I knew where I stood. It may have been grim at times but it was honest and you haven't been honest with me.' She swallowed. 'It feels like I'm in the shadows of your life—like someone in the wings watching the action on stage. I see the way you are with the baby—and with me—and it comes over as a performance, not real. How could it be, when Santino and I were only ever a means to an end?'

Matteo flinched as he met the accusation in her eyes, because nobody had ever spoken quite so candidly to him. 'For someone so tiny, you certainly don't pull any punches, do you, Keira?'

'What's the point in pulling punches? All we have left is the truth,' she said wearily. 'You've got what you wanted, Matteo. We're married now and your son has been legitimised. You have continued the Valenti name and will therefore inherit the estate. You don't need me any more.'

Matteo felt his chest tighten and his instinct was to tell her that she was right—and that he *didn't* need anyone. He'd spent his whole life not needing anyone because there had been nobody there to lean on, nobody to get close to—why change that pattern now? But some unknown emotion was nudging at his conscience as something deep inside him told him this was different.

'And what if I say I do need you?' he said hoarsely as he attempted to articulate the confusion of thoughts which were spinning around inside his head.

Her eyes widened, but he could see a wariness in their depths of *profondo blu*. 'You do?' she queried uncertainly.

The moment it took for her to ask the question was all Matteo needed to shift things into perspective, because he knew he mustn't offer her false promises or false hope. She deserved more than that. So stick to the facts, he urged himself grimly. You're good with facts. Allow her to consider all the advantages of remaining here, as his wife.

'Of course,' he said. 'And logistically it makes perfect sense.'

'Logistically?' she echoed, her voice a little faint.

'Sure.' He shrugged. 'If we're all living together under one roof as a family, it will be much better for Santino. Better than having a father who just jets in and sees him on high days and holidays.'

'There is that, of course,' she said woodenly.

'And I've married you now, Keira,' he said softly. 'I have given you the security of bearing my name and wearing my ring. Your future is assured. You don't need to worry about money ever again.'

'You think that's what it's all about?' she questioned, her voice trembling. 'Money?'

'Not all of it, no—but a big part of it. And we have plenty of other reasons to keep our marriage going.' He curved her a slow smile. 'What about the sexual chemistry which exists between us? That fact that you are the hottest woman I've ever had in my bed?'

She gasped as if she had been winded before staring at him—as if she were looking at someone she'd never seen before. 'You just don't get it, do you, Matteo? You list all the reasons I should stay with you and yet you haven't mentioned anything which really *matters*!'

He flinched with pain as he met the undiluted anger in her gaze, but at the same time a strange sense of relief washed over him as he realised that he no longer had to try. She was going and taking their child with him and he would just have to learn how to deal with that. And anyway, he thought grimly—why would he want to prolong a relationship when it could hurt like this? Hadn't he vowed never to let anyone hurt him, ever again?

'Okay, I get it. What do you want?'

With an effort he held up the palms of his hands, in silent submission, and the sudden wobble of her lips made him think she might be about to backtrack— maybe to soften the blows which she'd just rained on him, but all she said was, 'I'd like us to separate.'

He told himself it was better this way. Better to go back to the life he was used to and be the person he knew how to be, rather than chase after the glimmer of gold which Keira Ryan had brought shimmering into his life.

'Tell me what you want, in practical terms,' he said flatly.

He could see her throat constricting as she nodded.

'I'd like to return to London as soon as possible and to rent somewhere before I decide to buy,' she said, before sucking in a deep breath. 'But I want you to know that I'll take only what is necessary for our needs and you're not to worry. I don't intend to make a great hole in your wealth, Matteo.'

And even that got to him, because he couldn't even level the charge of greed against her. She wasn't interested in his money, he realised, and she never had been. She'd taken the cash he'd thoughtlessly left beside the bed and had given it away to charity. She'd fought like mad against him buying her a fancy wardrobe. She was a jewel of a woman, he realised—a bright and shining jewel. But it was too late for them. The cold, pinched look on her beautiful face told him that. So let her go, he told himself. Set her free. At least you can give her that.

'That can all be arranged,' he said. 'But in turn, I need your reassurance that I can continue to see my son.'

There was surprise on her face now and he wondered if secretly she had expected him to cut all ties with his own flesh and blood.

'Of course. You can see as much of Santino as you wish,' she said quietly. 'I will never deny you your son, Matteo, and I hope you will see him very often, because he...he needs you. You're his daddy.'

A lump rose in his throat as he moved away from the blaze of the fire.

'I'd like to say goodnight to him now,' he said and she nodded and made as if to follow him.

'Alone,' he gritted out.

But Matteo's heart was heavy as he walked towards the nursery—as if a dark stone had lodged itself deep inside his chest. The night light made the room appear soft and rosy and Matteo stared down at the sleeping child. He remembered the first time he had seen him. When he had counted his fingers and toes like someone learning basic mathematics, and had felt nothing.

But not this time.

This time he could barely make out any detail of his sleeping son, his vision was so blurred. Too late, his heart had cracked open and left room for emotion to come flooding in, powerfully and painfully. And Santino stirred as Matteo's tears fell like rain onto the delicate white shawl.

CHAPTER TWELVE

IT WAS RAINING by the time Keira got back from her walk and she had just let Charlie off his lead when she noticed the letter lying in the centre of the hall table, where Claudia must have left it. She pulled a face. Another one.

The envelope carried an Italian stamp and the airmail sticker seemed to wink at her. Quickly, she slid it into a drawer to lie on top of all the others, because she couldn't quite bring herself to throw them away. Her reluctance to dispose of the growing pile of correspondence was just about equal to her reluctance to read them, because they were from Matteo—she recognised his handwriting. And why would she wish to read them and risk making the hole in her heart even bigger? Why was he even *writing* to her when she'd told him it was better if all correspondence took place between their respective solicitors? Why had he arrogantly elected to take no notice?

Because she was fighting like crazy not to go under. Not to give into the tears which pricked at her eyes at night when she lay in bed missing the warm embrace

of her estranged husband. She was determined to pour
all her energies into being there for Santino—into being
the best mother she possibly could—and she couldn't
manage that if her heart stayed raw and aching from
thinking about Matteo all the time.

She'd wondered whether his determination to keep
in close contact with his son would have faded once
she and Santino had left Umbria but to her surprise, it
hadn't. He'd already paid two visits and they'd only been
back in England a little over a fortnight. On both those
occasions she had absented herself from the house, leaving Claudia in charge of the baby—Claudia who had
been happy to accompany her from Umbria when Keira
had made the emotional return to her homeland.

She supposed people might think it a form of cow-
ardice that she couldn't bear the thought of confronting
the man with whom she hadn't even shared a wedding
night. But that was too bad. It didn't matter what anyone else thought, only what was right for her and her
son. Sooner or later she hoped she'd be able to greet
him with a genuine air of indifference but for now she
didn't trust herself not to burst into noisy howls of sor-
row and to tell him how much she was missing him.

With the money he'd settled on her, she was rent-
ing a house. A house with a garden and a front door
which wasn't shared—the kind of house in Notting
Hill where she used to drop off her prep-school charges
when she was working at Luxury Limos. And she'd
bought a dog, too. A scruffy little thing with a lop-
sided ear and the saddest eyes she'd ever seen. The
staff at the rescue centre had told her he'd been badly

beaten and was fearful and shy, but he had taken one look at Keira and hurled himself at her with a series of plaintive yelps. Charlie was the best thing to have happened to them since they'd returned to England and had reinforced her intention to give Santino a proper childhood. The kind she'd never had—with a dog and a mother who was always waiting for him when he got home from school.

Pulling off her rain-soaked coat, she went upstairs to the nursery where Claudia was just putting Santino down to sleep. The nursery nurse straightened up as Keira entered the room and she found herself wondering why Claudia's cheeks were so pink. Walking over to the crib, Keira stared down into the sleepy eyes of her son, her heart turning over with love.

'He looks happy,' she murmured as she leaned over to plant a soft kiss on his silken cheek.

'He should be!' said Claudia. 'After you took him out for such a long walk this morning.'

'Good thing I did. At least we missed the rain,' said Keira, with an idle glance out of the window as she drew the curtains.

There was a pause. 'Would you mind if I went out earlier than planned?' asked Claudia.

'Of course I don't mind.' Keira smiled because she knew that Claudia had struck up a close friendship with a man she'd met at the Italian Embassy. 'Hot date?'

Claudia smiled as she put her forefinger over her lips and Keira was so preoccupied with tidying up the nursery that she barely registered the nursery nurse leaving the room, though she did hear the distant bang of the front door. She turned the light out and was just about to make her way downstairs when her mobile phone began to ring and she pulled it from the pocket of her jeans, frowning when she saw Matteo's name flashing up on the screen.

Fury began to bubble up inside her. She'd asked him not to write and he had ignored that. She'd asked him not to call her and he was ignoring that too! So why now, coming straight after yet another unwanted letter from him? She clicked the connection.

'This had better be urgent,' she said.

'It is.'

She frowned as she registered a curious echo-like quality to his voice. 'And?'

'I need to see you.'

She needed to see him too, but no good would come of it. Wouldn't it make her hunger for what she could never have and certainly didn't need—a man who had lured a woman into marriage just because he wanted to inherit a house? 'I thought we'd decided that wasn't a good idea.'

'No, Keira…*you* decided.'

Still that curious echo. Keira frowned. Shouldn't she just agree to see him once and get it over with? Steel her heart against her own foolish desires and listen to what he had to say? 'Very well,' she said. 'We'll put an appointment in the diary.'

'Now,' he bit out.

'What do you mean…*now*?'

'I want to see you now,' he growled.

'Matteo, you're in Italy and I'm in England and unless you've discovered the secret of teleportation, that's not going to happen.'

'I'm downstairs.'

She froze. '*What* did you say?'

'I'm downstairs.' The echo began to get louder. 'Coming up.'

Her heart slamming against her ribcage, Keira rushed from the nursery to see Matteo with his mobile phone held against his ear, making his way up the stairs towards her. His face was more serious than she'd ever seen it as he cut the connection and slid the phone into the pocket of his jeans.

'Hi,' he said, the casual greeting failing to hide the tension and the pain which were written across his ravaged features.

She wanted to do several things all at once. To drum her fists against his powerful chest, over and over again. And she wanted to pull his darkly handsome face to hers and kiss him until there was no breath left in her body.

'What are you doing here?' she demanded.

'I need to speak to you.'

'Did you have to go about it so dramatically? You scared me half to death!' She looked at him suspiciously. 'You don't have a key, do you?'

'I don't,' he agreed.

'So how did you get in?'

'Claudia let me in before she left.'

'Claudia let you in?' she repeated furiously. 'Why would she do something like that?'

'Because I asked her to.'

'And what you say goes, I suppose, because you're the one with the money,' she said contemptuously.

'No.' He sucked in a ragged breath. 'I'm the one with the broken heart.'

It was such an unbelievable thing for him to say that Keira assumed she'd misheard him, and she was too busy deciding that they needed to move out of Santino's earshot in case they woke him to pay very much attention to her husband's words. 'You'd better come with me,' she said.

Matteo followed the denim-covered sway of her bottom as they went downstairs, watching her long black ponytail swinging against her back with every determined stride she took. Her body language wasn't looking promising and neither was her attitude. But what had he expected—that she would squeal with delight when she saw him again? Welcome him into the embrace he had so missed—as if that whole great betrayal had never happened? His throat thickened. He had tried playing it slow and playing by her rules but he'd realised she would be prepared to push him away for ever if he let her.

And he couldn't afford to let her.

They reached a beautiful, high-ceilinged sitting room dominated by a tall Christmas tree, which glittered in front of one of the tall windows. Fragrant and green, it was covered with lights and tiny stars and on the top stood an angel with gossamer-fine wings. A heap of presents with ribbons and bows stood at the base of the giant conifer and Matteo thought it looked so homely. And yet he wasn't connected to any of it, was he? He was still the outsider. The motherless boy who had never really felt part of Christmas.

So what are you going to do about it, Valenti? he asked himself as she turned to face him and they stood looking at one another like two combatants.

'You wanted to talk,' she said, without preamble. 'So talk. Why did you sneak into my house like this?'

'You've been ignoring my letters.'

She nodded and the glossy black ponytail danced around her shoulders. 'I told you I wanted to keep all written communication between our respective solicitors.'

'You really think that my lawyer wants to hear that I love you?' he demanded, his breath a low hiss.

Her lips opened and he thought she might be about to gasp, before she closed them again firmly, like an oyster shell clamping tightly shut.

'And that I miss you more than I ever thought possible?' he continued heatedly. 'Or that my life feels empty without you?'

'Don't waste my time with your lies, Matteo.'

'They aren't lies,' he said unevenly. 'They're the truth.'

'I don't believe you.'

'I didn't think you would.' He sucked in a deep breath. 'Which is why I wrote you the letters.'

'The letters,' she repeated blankly.

'I know you got them, because I asked Claudia. What did you do with them, Keira—did you throw them away? Set light to them and watch them go up in flames?'

She shook her head. 'No. I didn't do that. I have them all.'

'Then, I wonder, could you possibly fetch them?'

Was it the word 'fetch' which brought Charlie bounding into the room, his tail wagging furiously and his once sad eyes bright and curious as he looked up at the strange man? Keira glared as she saw Matteo crouch down and offer his hand to the little dog, furious yet somehow unsurprised when the terrier edged cautiously towards him. The shock of seeing Matteo again had shaken her and weakened her defences, making her realise that she was still fundamentally shaky around him—and so she nodded her agreement to his bizarre request. At least leaving the room and his disturbing presence would give her the chance to compose herself and to quieten the fierce hammering of her heart.

Slowly she walked into the hallway to retrieve the pile of envelopes from the drawer and went back into the sitting room, holding them gingerly between her fingers, like an unexploded bomb. By now Charlie's tail was thrashing wildly, and as Matteo straightened up from stroking him the puppy gave a little whine of protest and she wondered how he had so quickly managed to charm the shy little dog. But the terrier had been discovered wriggling in a sack by the side of the road, she remembered, the only survivor among all his dead brothers and sisters. Charlie had also grown up without a mother, she thought—and a lump lodged in her throat.

'Here,' she croaked, holding the letters towards him.

'Don't you want to open them?' he said.

She shook her head. 'Not really.'

'Then maybe I'd better tell you what's in them,' he said, his eyes not leaving her face as he took them from her. 'They are all love letters. With the exception of one.'

He saw her eyes widen before dark lashes came shuttering down to cloak their sapphire hue with suspicion.

'What's that? A hate letter?' she quipped.

'I'm serious, Keira.'

'And so am I. Anyone can write down words on a piece of paper and not mean them.'

'Then how about I summarise them for you out loud?'

'No.'

But that one word was so whispered that he barely heard it and Matteo had no intention of heeding it anyway. 'Four words, actually,' he husked. 'I love you, Keira. So how about I say it again, just so there can be no misunderstanding? I love you, Keira, and I've been a fool. *Uno scemo!* I should have been honest with you from the start, but...' He inhaled deeply through his nostrils and then expelled the air on a shuddered breath. 'Keeping things locked away inside was the way I operated. The only way I knew. But believe me when I tell you that by the time I asked you to marry me, I wasn't thinking about the house any more. My mind was full of you. It still is. I can't stop thinking about you and I don't want to. So I'm asking you to give me another chance, Keira. To give *us* another chance. You, me and Santino. That's all.'

She didn't say anything for a moment and when she spoke she started shaking her head, as if what he was demanding of her was impossible.

'That's *all*?' she breathed. 'After everything that's happened? You don't know what you're asking, Matteo.'

'Oh, but I do,' he demurred. 'I'm asking you to be my wife for real. With nothing but total honesty between us from now on, because I want that. I want that more than anything.' His voice lowered. 'But I realise it can only work if you love me too. Once, in a shadowed hallway after we had taken our wedding vows, you whispered to me that you did, but you may not have meant it.'

Keira clamped her lips together to try to contain the stupid tremble of emotion. Of course she had meant it. Every single word. The question was whether he did, too. Was it possible that he really loved her, or was this simply a means to an end—the manipulative declaration of a man determined to get his rightful heir back into his life? Or maybe just pride refusing to let a woman walk away from him.

Yet something was stubbornly refusing to allow her to accept the bleaker version of his reasons for coming here today. Was it the anguish she could see in his black eyes—so profound that even she, in her insecurity, didn't believe she was imagining it? She flicked the tip of her tongue over her mouth, wondering if it was too late for them, until she realised what the reality of that would mean. Matteo gone from her life and free to make another with someone else, while she would never be able to forget him.

And she wasn't going to allow that to happen. Because how could she ignore the burning inside her heart and the bright spark of hope which was beginning to flood through her veins?

'I've tried not to love you,' she admitted slowly. 'But it doesn't work. I think about you nearly all the time and I miss you. I love you, Matteo, and I will be your wife, but on one condition.'

His body grew very still. 'Anything,' he said. 'Name it.'

She had been about to ask him never knowingly to hurt her, but she realised that was all part of the package. That hurt and pain were the price you paid for love and you just had to pray they didn't rear their bitter heads too often in a lifetime. She knew also that if they wanted to go forward, then they had to leave the bitterness of the past behind. So instead of demanding the impossible, she touched her fingertips to his face, tracing them slowly down over his cheek until they came to rest on his beautiful lips.

'That you make love to me,' she said, her voice softened by tears of joy. 'And convince me this really is happening.'

His voice was unsteady. 'You mean, right now?'

She swallowed and nodded, rapidly wiping underneath her eyes with a bent finger. 'This very second,' she gulped.

Framing her face within the palms of his hands, he looked at her for one long moment before he spoke. 'To the woman who has given me everything, because without you I am nothing. *Ti amo, mia sposa.* My beautiful, beautiful wife,' he husked, and crushed his lips down hard on hers.

EPILOGUE

OUTSIDE THE WINDOW big white flakes floated down from the sky, adding to the dazzling carpet which had already covered the vast sweep of lawn. Keira gazed at it and gave a dreamy sigh. It was unusual for snow to settle in this part of Umbria and she thought she'd never seen anything quite so magical, or so beautiful. She smiled. Well, except maybe one other time...

Looking up from where she was crouched beside the Christmas tree where she'd just placed a couple of presents, she saw Matteo walk into the room—with snowflakes melting against his dark hair. He'd been outside, putting the finishing touches to a snowman, which would be the first thing Santino saw when he looked out of his window tomorrow morning. Their son's first real Christmas, Keira thought, because last year he'd been too young to realise what was going on and she...

Well, if she was being honest, she could hardly remember last Christmas herself. She and Matteo had been busy discovering each other all over again—and finding out that things were different from how they'd been before. They couldn't have been anything *but* different once the constraints of the past were lifted and they'd given themselves the freedom to say exactly what was on their minds. Or in their hearts.

Matteo had given her the option of living in London, Rome or Umbria—and she'd opted for the sprawling Umbrian estate which had once belonged to his mother's family. She figured it was healthier for Santino to grow up in the glorious Italian countryside, especially now that they had acquired a beautiful black cat named Luca who, against all odds, had become a devoted companion to Charlie the terrier.

But it was more than that. This estate was Matteo's link with his roots. It represented continuity and stability—something which had been lacking in both their lives until now. One day Santino might listen to the call of his forebears and decide he didn't want to be a businessman, like his daddy. He might want to grow up and farm the fertile acres of this beautiful place. A place which might so nearly have disappeared from the family.

Because Keira had discovered that the very first letter Matteo had sent during their separation contained estate agent details marketing the property. He'd put it up for sale to demonstrate that the house meant nothing, if he didn't have her. They had quickly aborted the prospective sale, despite the frantic bidding war which had been taking place at the time. And had decided to make the estate their permanent home.

'What are you smiling at?' questioned Matteo softly as he walked over to the Christmas tree and pulled her to her feet.

Her contented expression didn't change. 'Do I need a reason?' She sighed. 'I'm just so happy, Matteo. Happier than I ever thought possible.'

'Well, isn't that a coincidence? Because I feel exactly the same way,' he said, his fingers beginning to massage her shoulders, their practised caress never failing to arouse her. 'Have I told you lately that I love you, Mrs Valenti?'

She pretended to frown. 'I think you might have mentioned it before you went out to build Santino's snowman. And just for the record, I love you, too. So very much.'

He bent his head and kissed her, deeply and passionately and it was some time before she broke off to graze her lips against the dark stubble of his angled jaw.

'Did you speak to your father?' she said.

'I did. And he's looking forward to Christmas lunch tomorrow. He says he'll be here soon after eleven and is bringing his new girlfriend.' His eyes gleamed down at her. 'And that we should prepare ourselves for what he calls a *significant* age gap.'

Keira giggled as she rested her head on Matteo's shoulder. Massimo had divorced Luciana in the spring and although Keira had tried to feel sad about it, she just couldn't. Not only had the older woman been a troublemaker—it transpired that she'd been unfaithful to her husband as well. And one night, soon after the decree nisi had come through and Matteo had been away on business, Keira and her father-in-law had dined together in Rome. He'd told her it wasn't a desire to manipulate which had made him threaten to disinherit Matteo if he didn't produce an heir—but concern that his son was becoming emotionally remote and would end up a rich and lonely old man.

'And then you stepped in and saved him and made him happy. Truly happy—and I cannot thank you enough for that, Keira,' he had whispered, his voice cracking a little. 'I know I wasn't a good father when he was growing up.' He had fallen silent for a moment and his eyes had grown reflective. 'I missed his mother so much and he…well, he looked so much like her, that sometimes it was painful to be around him.'

'Have you told him that, Massimo?' she had said quietly, pressing her hand over his across the table. 'Because I think you should.'

And he had. Keira closed her eyes, remembering the long overdue heart-to-heart between father and son, and the growing closeness of their relationship which had resulted.

Her mind flicked back to the present as Matteo began to caress her bottom, murmuring his appreciation that these days she almost always wore a dress. She liked wearing dresses, although she could still resurrect her inner tomboy when needed—and she suspected she was going to need to do that a lot if Santino played as much football as Matteo intended he should. 'Would you like part of your Christmas present tonight?' she whispered, snuggling up to him.

He pulled away to look at her and raised his eyebrows. 'Is that an offer I shouldn't refuse?'

'Put it this way—I'm wearing it underneath this dress and I need you to unwrap it for me. Matteo!' She giggled as he began to lead her towards the bedroom. 'I didn't mean *now*—I meant later.'

'Too bad,' he murmured, not lessening his pace by a fraction. 'Because I have something for you which can't wait.'

Actually, that wasn't quite true—he had two things for her. The first was sitting in the garage wrapped in a giant red bow ready to be untied on Christmas morning. A neglected Ferrari 1948 Spider sports car which he'd tracked down with great difficulty and at considerable expense, because she'd once told him it was her dream to restore beautiful vintage cars—and Matteo was rather partial to making his wife's dreams come true.

The second gift was rather different and he didn't give it to her until after he'd dealt with her outrageous panty thong with its matching boned bodice, which he damaged beyond repair in his eagerness to unhook it. And once he had her naked, he was distracted for quite some time...

His throat thickened with unexpected emotion as he pulled the small box from his discarded trousers and flipped open the lid to reveal a flawless white solitaire which sparkled like a giant star against dark velvet.

'What's this?' she questioned breathlessly, from among the sheets which were rumpled around her.

He lifted her left hand and slid the solitaire in place above her wedding band. 'I never gave you an engagement ring, did I? And I didn't give you a dream wedding either. A civil ceremony in a town hall was never something we were going to enjoy telling our grandchildren about.' He lifted her hand to his lips and kissed her fingertips. 'So I wondered if you'd like to renew our vows in my favourite church in Rome. You could wear a big white dress and do it properly this time, and we could throw a party afterwards. Or not—whichever you prefer. What I'm asking is, would you like to marry me again, Keira Valenti?'

Keira opened her mouth to say that she didn't care about pomp or ceremony, but that wasn't quite true. And weren't she and Matteo all about the truth, these days? She thought about something else, too, something which had been niggling away at her for a while now. Because weddings could bring people together and heal old wounds, couldn't they? Motherhood had changed her. Softened her. She realised now that her aunt might have been strict when she was growing up, but she'd given an orphaned little girl the home she'd badly needed and had stopped her from being taken into care. And didn't she owe her aunt Ida a great deal for that? Wasn't it time to invite her and Shelley to Italy, to share in her good fortune and happiness and to introduce Santino to some of *her* roots?

She wound her arms around Matteo's neck and looked into his beautiful black eyes, her heart turning over with emotion. 'Yes, Matteo,' she said breathlessly. 'I'll be proud to marry you. To stand before our family and friends and say the thing I'll never tire of saying, which is that I love you—and I'll love you for the rest of my life.'

* * * * *

MILLS & BOON®
Hardback – November 2017

ROMANCE

The Italian's Christmas Secret	Sharon Kendrick
A Diamond for the Sheikh's Mistress	Abby Green
The Sultan Demands His Heir	Maya Blake
Claiming His Scandalous Love-Child	Julia James
Valdez's Bartered Bride	Rachael Thomas
The Greek's Forbidden Princess	Annie West
Kidnapped for the Tycoon's Baby	Louise Fuller
A Night, A Consequence, A Vow	Angela Bissell
Christmas with Her Millionaire Boss	Barbara Wallace
Snowbound with an Heiress	Jennifer Faye
Newborn Under the Christmas Tree	Sophie Pembroke
His Mistletoe Proposal	Christy McKellen
The Spanish Duke's Holiday Proposal	Robin Gianna
The Rescue Doc's Christmas Miracle	Amalie Berlin
Christmas with Her Daredevil Doc	Kate Hardy
Their Pregnancy Gift	Kate Hardy
A Family Made at Christmas	Scarlet Wilson
Their Mistletoe Baby	Karin Baine
The Texan Takes a Wife	Charlene Sands
Twins for the Billionaire	Sarah M. Anderson

MILLS & BOON®
Large Print – November 2017

ROMANCE

The Pregnant Kavakos Bride	Sharon Kendrick
The Billionaire's Secret Princess	Caitlin Crews
Sicilian's Baby of Shame	Carol Marinelli
The Secret Kept from the Greek	Susan Stephens
A Ring to Secure His Crown	Kim Lawrence
Wedding Night with Her Enemy	Melanie Milburne
Salazar's One-Night Heir	Jennifer Hayward
The Mysterious Italian Houseguest	Scarlet Wilson
Bound to Her Greek Billionaire	Rebecca Winters
Their Baby Surprise	Katrina Cudmore
The Marriage of Inconvenience	Nina Singh

HISTORICAL

Ruined by the Reckless Viscount	Sophia James
Cinderella and the Duke	Janice Preston
A Warriner to Rescue Her	Virginia Heath
Forbidden Night with the Warrior	Michelle Willingham
The Foundling Bride	Helen Dickson

MEDICAL

Mummy, Nurse...Duchess?	Kate Hardy
Falling for the Foster Mum	Karin Baine
The Doctor and the Princess	Scarlet Wilson
Miracle for the Neurosurgeon	Lynne Marshall
English Rose for the Sicilian Doc	Annie Claydon
Engaged to the Doctor Sheikh	Meredith Webber

)17 GEN STD LP

MILLS & BOON®
Hardback – December 2017

ROMANCE

His Queen by Desert Decree	Lynne Graham
A Christmas Bride for the King	Abby Green
Captive for the Sheikh's Pleasure	Carol Marinelli
Legacy of His Revenge	Cathy Williams
A Night of Royal Consequences	Susan Stephens
Carrying His Scandalous Heir	Julia James
Christmas at the Tycoon's Command	Jennifer Hayward
Innocent in the Billionaire's Bed	Clare Connelly
Snowed in with the Reluctant Tycoon	Nina Singh
The Magnate's Holiday Proposal	Rebecca Winters
The Billionaire's Christmas Baby	Marion Lennox
Christmas Bride for the Boss	Kate Hardy
Christmas with the Best Man	Susan Carlisle
Navy Doc on Her Christmas List	Amy Ruttan
Christmas Bride for the Sheikh	Carol Marinelli
Her Knight Under the Mistletoe	Annie O'Neil
The Nurse's Special Delivery	Louisa George
Her New Year Baby Surprise	Sue MacKay
His Secret Son	Brenda Jackson
Best Man Under the Mistletoe	Jules Bennett

MILLS & BOON®
Large Print – November 2017

ROMANCE

An Heir Made in the Marriage Bed	Anne Mather
The Prince's Stolen Virgin	Maisey Yates
Protecting His Defiant Innocent	Michelle Smart
Pregnant at Acosta's Demand	Maya Blake
The Secret He Must Claim	Chantelle Shaw
Carrying the Spaniard's Child	Jennie Lucas
A Ring for the Greek's Baby	Melanie Milburne
The Runaway Bride and the Billionaire	Kate Hardy
The Boss's Fake Fiancée	Susan Meier
The Millionaire's Redemption	Therese Beharrie
Captivated by the Enigmatic Tycoon	Bella Bucannon

HISTORICAL

Marrying His Cinderella Countess	Louise Allen
A Ring for the Pregnant Debutante	Laura Martin
The Governess Heiress	Elizabeth Beacon
The Warrior's Damsel in Distress	Meriel Fuller
The Knight's Scarred Maiden	Nicole Locke

MEDICAL

Healing the Sheikh's Heart	Annie O'Neil
A Life-Saving Reunion	Alison Roberts
The Surgeon's Cinderella	Susan Carlisle
Saved by Doctor Dreamy	Dianne Drake
Pregnant with the Boss's Baby	Sue MacKay
Reunited with His Runaway Doc	Lucy Clark

✶MILLS & BOON®

Why shop at millsandboon.co.uk?

Each year, thousands of romance readers find their
perfect read at millsandboon.co.uk. That's because
we're passionate about bringing you the very best
romantic fiction. Here are some of the advantages
of shopping at www.millsandboon.co.uk:

✶ **Get new books first**—you'll be able to buy your
  favourite books one month before they hit
  the shops

✶ **Get exclusive discounts**—you'll also be able to buy
  our specially created monthly collections, with up
  to 50% off the RRP

✶ **Find your favourite authors**—latest news,
  interviews and new releases for all your favourite
  authors and series on our website, plus ideas for
  what to try next

✶ **Join in**—once you've bought your favourite books,
  don't forget to register with us to rate, review and
  join in the discussions

Visit **www.millsandboon.co.uk**
for all this and more today!